THE MOMENTS YOU MISS

THE WHISPERING SERIES
BOOK ONE

MAE ROBERTS

ISBN-13: 979-8-9991248-2-1

Cover design by: @heygigicreatives

Editor: Michele L. Manuel

Formatting: Mae Roberts

To the ones who love fucked up shit but still love that Happily Ever After. This isn't that book.
Everyone dies.

TRIGGER WARNINGS

This is a DARK romance, these are triggers that are included in this book, including but not limited to:

Death of a Family Member
Castration/Removal of Penis
Torture (physical and emotional)
Sexual Assault (mentioned, not seen)
Grief
Kidnapping
General Violence
Non-Consensual Kissing
Murder
Blood/Gore
Stalking
Mention of Enucleation

Strangulation

Blood

PTSD

Self - Harm (Not depicted, only mention of scars)

PROLOGUE

October 21st, what a great fucking day for someone to die.

It's colder than it should be for this time of year, making the night air *crisp* and just right. I slam the door shut and yell out for my apprentice to join me. I know that they're young, but idle hands make for poor choices. I have a job: I rid the world of those who do the inexcusable, unforgivable, and deplorable.

I'm not a good person, nor have I ever fucking claimed to be.

We hop into the car, and I know that what we're about to do will change the outcome for a lot of things in the future. I know that my apprentice is terrified, and they need to fucking learn that they're growing up, and they can't be this pathetic waste of space for much longer.

"Explain to me again exactly what we're going to be doing." I pull the pack of cigarettes, tapping the box on the palm of my hand, flicking my zippo, and lighting it with a deep inhale. The taste of cheap tobacco always brings me back to these moments, leading up to the kill. It's almost nostalgic for me.

The voice of my apprentice echoes through the cab of my truck. "Richard Clarkson, predator, has..." their throat wobbles, knowing that this isn't a conversation they want to be having but I don't fucking care.

"Keep fucking going." I growl, as the voice continues.

"Richard is a predator; kidnapped and tortured at least six women, suspected at least eight more, with not much evidence to go on." They look up at me, wanting something that they won't get; approval, acceptance, praise. Not from me. It's a short drive to the little town where this monster lives; he lives off the beaten path which makes my fucking job that much easier. Their end is coming.

The mother is an unfortunate piece of collateral damage that I have no problem closing out, using their child as bait to kidnap these women. Richard is-was a monster of a man, and his life has to come to an end. This is a burden I happily bear. I turn to my accomplice– giving them a nod as they hand me my kit.

A wicked smile grows on my face as I watch as the two cower in the corner, whimpering and begging for mercy. The couple is frozen as I begin to tie the two of them up. Neither of them fights back, knowing that they truly don't have a chance of getting out of here. I walk up to the wife, Sheila Clarkson, the mother who used their own child for personal gain. The fact that the child is nowhere to be found has left a nagging feeling of untied loose ends that could bite us in the ass.

His wife lets out a scream, I throw her a withering glare and her voice quiets. I see her looking to the side, trying to be inconspicuous. "Looking for someone?"

Sheila's red hair is mussed and matted, she looks disheveled, and her face is streaked with tears. She whimpers and shakes her head.

"I don't do well with liars." My lips touch the shell of her ear; her body reacts with a whole-body shiver, knowing my threat is hitting the mark. I turn to my apprentice, urging them to watch carefully. "Like this," I whisper with another grimace on my face as I grab the woman's hair, pulling her hair back with force.

"Where is she?" I growl.

The woman stammers away, trying to talk through the gag we had placed in their mouths. "No-not– no– please," Sheila Clarkson pleads as she attempts to wriggle out of my grasp. When she manages to get the gag out of her mouth just slightly, my eyes gleam as I see the fear settle into her. Acceptance hits her; and before she can come to terms with what is actually happening, I smirk as I look at my apprentice.

"Useless," I tut before slashing the knife along her throat and the gurgles escape as she falls silent.

A quiet voice comes up behind me, and I turn to my apprentice. Their eyes bug out as they watch the blood pool beneath the corpse. The man tied up next to her, screams and thrashes unsuccessfully.

"Hallway. *Now*," I order my apprentice; they follow behind.

"*Kill him*." I don't even give a moment to respond. "I'm running to the car. That man better not be alive by the time I get back in here you understand me?" I grab them by the collar of their shirt, a soft whimper escapes them and I throw them off; they lose their balance but quickly set themself straight. Their hands are white knuckling the knife I gave them, and they head off to the room and I head out to the car.

Five minutes later, I walk back in the room, and find two dead bodies. One by me. One by them.

"Good kid," I say, the first true morsel of praise I've ever given them. "Help me move them." My head motioning to the two dead bodies. We position them up on the bed, as if they're sleeping. This is my M.O., this is what I am training them to do.

The Whispering Killer has indeed struck again, cleansing the world of the darkness.

PART ONE

1

FLASHING LIGHTS
LEYLA -- 10 YEARS OLD, 12 YEARS AGO

The lights are really bright, and I don't like it. My brain is really fuzzy right now and I can't think straight. I'm not really sure what's going on, but the lady with the green eyes said that my Mommy and Daddy aren't coming back, but I already knew that. I saw them in bed last night. The man said they can't hurt anyone anymore, so they're sleeping forever. The police lady said that I'm gonna go with her to the station, then they'll get me a new teddy bear or some other plushie. I really don't know why I would need a teddy.

A few hours pass and I'm sitting in the station and they're giving me some snacks. Mommy never let me eat them at home, so I'm really excited over the cookies and chips. They are even better than I imagined! Sweet, salty, crunchy, *mmm*.

They seem worried that I'm not crying or talking. Daddy always told me never to tell anyone what they did and I'm really good at listening to directions. The detective, that's the lady from my house, keeps asking me questions, but she's really nice. She wants to know more about Mommy and Daddy, I will not tell! It's mine and Daddy's secret.

When my Daddy would go on his trips he always came home, and he would always take me to visit our favorite spot in the woods with all the pretty stones. Daddy said this is where the bad people he knows go. I really loved my Daddy, even if daddy wasn't a good man. That's what Mommy would always say. We love him even if he's bad, because he's ours.

———

I think it's been a while now. I took a nap on the couch at the police station and the detective came back after talking to her friends. She pulled out her chair and sat down in front of me. The crayons and paper scatter around the table. It's a picture of Daddy and Mommy.

"How are you feeling, Sweetie?" Detective Alexandra Harris smiles wide at me.

I shrug, not really sure how to feel. I just know I don't want to talk to anyone. Sitting in the Michigan State Police Department is overwhelming, and it's loud. My eyes connect with her, my body shivers slightly as her concerned gaze envelops me. Her stare feels like a warm hug that I don't deserve. The feeling of suddenly needing to find somewhere else to look overcomes me. I stare at a pile of papers behind her on the corner of a desk for some time, everything around me becoming a vacuum. I think I hear someone say something, my name maybe, then I feel a hand on my shoulder. I jump in my seat, everyone is looking up at me, but words won't form.

Detective Alexandra turns to her partner and whispers, "Has she said a single word this entire time?"

The man shakes his head, and responds back, "Not a word, not even when she was given toys and a tablet."

Detective Alexandra says, "We need her to talk, and talk soon, we've got social services coming in the next few hours, and they're gonna send her off to an emergency placement. I'm really worried that she's still in shock."

I sit in the chair just looking up at the two of them, my little hands grasping the red crayon. I lean forward and start tugging on her shirt, shoving the artwork to her. I just want them to like my pretty picture. The picture is of my parents, lying in their bed. Their eyes are black, just like the real thing. I saw that their eyes were plucked from their heads and placed in their hands. The eyes looked like they were watching me.

My body shivers as that memory comes back to my brain. The scene was so scary, and I saw it all. The two officers clearly aren't a fan of my picture, because Detective Alexandra's face looks all funny. She is pale and red climbs up her cheeks, then she shakes her head and puts on a pretty smile as she walks towards me.

"Hey-hey kiddo, what did you draw?" Alexandra asks sweetly, trying to get me to talk to her, or just at all. I urge the drawing into her hands, pointing to the picture. Detective Alexandra frowns as she looks at me. "Oh, Leyla." The detective's hand cups my cheek.

I flinch but then look up at her, my big eyes connecting with hers. I just shrug as a disappointed look takes over my face as she hands the picture off to the other detective, speaking in hushed whispers. My lips purse as I start to say something, but they're too busy talking to each other.

———

A few more hours pass, and Detective Alexandra comes walking out of her office towards me. I shoot up to stand, my eyes darting up as I look at her, my fingers pattering away on the table. I'm *so bored*. I still haven't cried yet, but Daddy said, *"No crying for my little spitfire."*

Daddy always told me I'm a big girl and that I need to be big and strong because the world's a scary place. My brows scrunch as I watch Detective Alexandra squat down in front of me. A lady with a backpack comes in, I think they told me her name, but I hadn't bothered to pay attention to it.

"Hey Leyla, my name's Miss Elizabeth, I'm here to take you to a fun new place where some really nice people will take care of you, okay?" I tilt my head back as I look over Miss Elizabeth. My hand shoots out to grasp hers and I jump out of the chair, I want to get out of this place, it's scary.

"Eager little one, I see!" Elizabeth laughs and she lets me hold her hand tightly, as if this would all fade away were I to let go. I'm scared, *really* scared but I know that this will be okay. Detective Alexandra looks down at me again and hands me a little backpack with some unicorns on it, and I love unicorns. I quickly put the backpack on and give her a slight smile, nodding aggressively as if saying thank you. The two adults walk away leaving me alone again as I stand outside the office. They're doing paperwork and obviously talking about me.

"She hasn't said a word?" Miss Elizabeth asks Detective Alexandra, the two of them trying to be quiet while I stand outside the door fiddling with the strap of the pretty new backpack they gave me.

"Not a word. Her parents were murdered, and I think she's gone into shock, but she's a sweet girl. I left my number in her backpack, and I wrote up a report. I need it known that when she does start talking, we will need a statement."

I watch as they finish their conversation, then Miss Elizabeth walks out and takes my hand. As we walk away from the police station, I hold on real tight, and she gives my hand a firm squeeze.

"Let's go, sweetheart." Her voice is soft as she gives my hand another squeeze, gentler this time. I keep my eyes ahead as she takes me to my new home. I *really* hope they like me.

2

GROUP THERAPY
CAMERON 16/ LEYLA 14 — 8 YEARS AGO

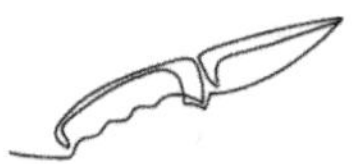

"Um... Hi, my name is Leyla, I'm fourteen."

I watch as she bites her lip nervously, her hands kept firmly at her sides. Leyla's hands wring themselves into white knuckled fists. Her anxiety and fear wafting off her, and it breaks my heart. Everyone who has grown up in Maplewood knows that story. Knows *her* story.

Our therapist has always told us that talking about what we've gone through will make moving on easier. Leyla looks like she's about to cry when the small, curly-haired girl places her hand in hers, and gives it a squeeze. It's as if the girl's presence gives Leyla the nudge she needs to go on.

"My parents were killed when I was ten, and I was put in... Well, I've been in foster care since I was ten too." My brows furrow as I listen intently to her greeting.

"Thank you, Leyla, thank you for trusting us with your story." The therapist smiles sweetly, her black rimmed glasses that are two times too big for her face falling down the bridge of her nose.

She's been coming to the group for at least two months now, and I haven't worked up the courage to talk to her. But today's going to be the day. I feel it in my bones.

Leyla's parents were killed in a way that for most would be a thing of nightmares. It was a night that she lives through every day, and it's written across her sweet face, the pain that she must feel.

I owe my life to her, I owe who I am, but she doesn't know me; and yet, I know everything there is to know about Leyla. Today is the day, our fate is finally happening, we are *finally* going to become a part of each other's lives. I'll repay her in a million ways for the kindness she doesn't even remember. But I remember, and I'll never forget.

I watch as red hair falls down her back in ringlets and I can't help but notice she's got really pretty eyes. One of her eyes is this arctic blue color, while her other eye is a turquoise green. I've never seen someone as pretty as her.

The thought of what that night was like for her, my back stiffens, my eyes widen, and breath as the fear of what she must have gone through hits me. I let the feeling fall off of me, knowing that this isn't happening now; it happened so long ago. *The only one who deserves my attention is her. I owe it all to her.*

I've seen her around school keeping to herself, this is the first time I've actually heard her talk. She tends to be very quiet. We all knew her story though. Well, *I* know her story. I already know everything there is to possibly know about her that can be found on the general world wide web. I promise there's nothing weird going on there. I just really like to know who people are, especially when they've got interesting stories.

I know she's meant for more. I am going to be the one to help her– I just need to talk to her first. My dad tells me that I'm only sixteen and I'm thinking with my hormones around most girls, but none of the girls in school are *her*. I'm gonna marry her someday.

We all sit around in a circle and this quack of a therapist talks to all of us, but my eyes never stray from Leyla Clarkson. *She's so fucking pretty.* The other guys in the group clearly all have the same idea, staring at her as if she's a piece of meat.

———

We're all dismissed after group and most of the others usually hang around talking and eating the shitty snacks that are left over. Normally, I bolt the second I can, but today I find myself lingering, picking at the table, just waiting for my turn to talk to her. I *will* talk to her. I walk over to my friends and angle myself so I can get a good look at her.

"Dude, she's so hot. Right?" Ryann, one of the other boys, says as he shoves some chips into his mouth

"She's not hot, she's beautiful," Simon corrects quietly. Both Ryann and I turn our attention to Simon, his shaggy black hair, unkept and messy falling in front of his eyes as we hear a melodic laugh come from her direction. Everyone in group knows that Simon has always been obsessed with Leyla since the moment she joined. Simon's eyes never leave Leyla; he bites his lip so hard at times as he's watching her, that it starts bleeding. My blood boils at the thought of someone else looking at her in such a claiming way.

"I-I had to switch to a different math class, because I was failing." Simon's voice echoes around us, as he tries to interject himself into a conversation that we really don't want to join.

Ryann's face scrunches and he rolls his eyes, "Aren't you like, really good at math?"

Simon replies, his eyes, the color of pitch, still never leaving Leyla's general direction. "Leyla's in my class too, w-we sit near each other. Sh-She's so smart so I know that I'll be really good at this c-class with h-her help."

My voice is tighter than intended, clearing my throat I look to Simon. "You... switched classes to be in the same class as her? Simon, that's fucking weird."

An insinuation that he tries to dismiss, stammering, "N-NO! No... she just... she's just in the same... same class as me!" Simon runs his hand through his messy black hair.

"Yea... Okay... You're so fucking strange." My attention is captured by a flash of Leyla's red hair in the sunlight. She stands by a table, her laughter changing to a soft lilt as she talks to another girl. I take a breath as I hear it and let it settle in my bones. *She's perfect.*

As nonchalantly as I can, I make my way over to her and I'm positive that this is gonna go perfectly. Simon tries to say something to me, but I'm already turning away from the table to make my way over to Leyla with this newfound confidence that I only seem to have when it has to do with her.

"Hi," I say as I walk up as she leans on the table, deep in

conversation with her friend. Her eyes widen as she looks at me in surprise, though it quickly turns to curiosity. I can tell by the way she wrinkles her brow as she angles away from me to keep talking to her friend. I clear my throat, and her eyes widen just slightly.

Those eyes that are engraved on my psyche. My memory. *My heart.*

"I said, 'hi'," I speak up a little more clearly now, a confidence coming off me that I definitely do not have. Maybe she just didn't hear me. Her body turns toward me, quirking a brow and crossing her arms as she assesses me.

"Uh, hi?" Leyla laughs as she side-eyes her friend, Hazel Mathis.

"I'm Cameron. Do you wanna hang out?" I smile nervously as I speak to her, beginning to worry that I'm absolutely tanking this conversation. Leyla giggles as she whispers something to her friend, leaning away from me; and for that moment, I ache. Then, her friend whispers something in return and Leyla turns back to me and shrugs.

"Okay, yea, I guess?"

The smile on my face is definitely too large to be casual. I can't help it, it's Leyla after all. My hand runs through my hair nervously. "I'm Cameron."

Leyla's face scrunches. "Yeah, you said that." She eyes me for a long, almost devastating moment before speaking to her friend without turning her way. "I'll talk to you later, Hazel."

———

Cameron and I walk towards the park nearby. Miss Kira won't be here to pick me up for at least another twenty-five minutes so what's the worst thing that could happen? Hazel told me that Cameron's mom was killed too and that he was also a foster kid. Pretty sure he's not actually one, but I really don't know the guy. And my therapist said making friends is something I need to work on.

I shoot Cameron an awkward smile. I was diagnosed with Selective Mutism in the months following my parents' murder, so having normal conversations with someone I don't know isn't something I'm really good at. It's like my brain wants to talk, but the words just don't come out. But he seems nice enough that I can give it a shot.

We walk over to the swings and sit down next to each other, he looks towards me and smiles really wide again.

"Sorry for being so awkward. My therapist says I need to be better about talking to people." He looks over at me as if that would make this interaction any less uncomfortable. I smile nevertheless, looking over the kid with the nerd glasses that decided that today I would be his next victim.

"Oh, it's cool. So, how long have you been in the group?" I ask, trying to make small talk.

I notice it then, the tension in the air; only it's not angry or actually tense? I can't seem to put my finger on it. It seems to be a charged feeling between us as we talk. As though each word, while intentional and awkward, is heavy and fateful. It's clear that he feels it too, at least I think since he's watching me so closely and his eyes so wide. The hair on the back of my neck stands up.

"Sorry, I- sorry..." he stammers out, as I look at him with gentle eyes.

"You really don't have to keep apologizing, we can just talk? I promise I don't bite." The rest of our conversation goes on without a hitch after that. He is actually pretty funny and seems super nice; maybe making friends isn't the worst thing that could happen to me.

The two of us talk for a while before there is a car honking nearby and his face goes two shades paler than I'd ever seen.

"Oh-Oh. Well, that's my ride— I'll see you next week?"

"Yea, see you next week. Save me a spot."

Maybe talking to Cameron isn't such a bad thing. My therapist told me I need to "expand my surroundings". So that's what I'm doing. At least, that's what I'm telling myself as I watch him hurry across the grass toward the waiting car.

Why are my cheeks hurting?

3
HEY YOU
CAMERON 18/ LEYLA 16 — 6 YEARS AGO

My dad screams at me; the painful words never get easier. He's starting to lose his memories more and more every single day, but it doesn't mean he's changed. My fucking black eye is a stark reminder that I'll never be good enough for my dad, and that he will constantly get away with every fucking thing he's ever done because of who he is.

I stare at him while he sits in that stupid recliner with a toothpick in his mouth, watching his shows. I know now that it's not *all* his fault that he's like this, but I'm only eighteen. It's not like I *have* to be here, but I feel as though I owe it to him to take care of him; I suppose that's what even the loosest sense of family does to you. At least I did until he started talking nonsense. Plus, with me going off to college soon, it's better if I get dad the help he needs. One less thing to weigh on my conscience.

"Dad– Hey, Dad–" I try to keep my voice lower, not wanting to agitate him any further. He looks at me confused, as if he's trying to make sense of who I am.

"Dad, it's me. Cameron… let's get you dressed to go to the doctor's, okay?" My voice is deceptively soft as he furrows his brows, the anger closing in on me as I take a step back.

"Cameron…" he echoes. For a moment, I think he's with me. But then his eyes grow hazy and distant. "Cameron, that boy… He's my piece of shit son, do you know where he is?"

Okay, he's clearly not fully with it today. I've learned that when he's like this, to just play it off as though I'm someone else. It's easier on him, and less of a chance for him to beat the shit out of me.

"I'm sure he's gonna come by later. Let's get this jacket on you so we can get you to the doctor, okay?"

Dad scans my face, trying to figure out if he can trust me or not, but relents when I start putting the jacket on him. Little does he know, he won't be coming back to this house ever again. I wish I had it in me to be upset over this, but I know deep down, taking my dad to a memory assisted-living place will be the best thing for him.

He mutters that he *'needs to take a wiz before we get going'* and shuffles off to the bathroom. Knowing that it's going to take a few minutes for him to get in the car, I pull out my phone and call Leyla, who's probably just getting out of school for the day.

"Hey, you." My voice is deceptively calm, but we've been hanging out every so often for the past couple of years. She's been the one who can always calm me down, who can make things not seem as shitty.

"Cameron?" Leyla's sweet voice floats through my phone speaker, my eyes narrowing at the bathroom door. I can feel myself holding my breath to listen closer to the sounds of him being done in there, even though I don't mean to. Habits die hard when they are built for survival.

"You okay, Cammy?" Leyla asks when I take too long to reply.

"I'm– I'm uh, taking my dad to assisted living today and I just needed to hear your voice," I admit, my hand runs through my definitely too long hair.

"Oh, I'm sorry to hear that." Even though it's just mere words that anyone could say, Leyla's voice settles through me like a balm to an open wound that won't stop bleeding. "I know you two don't have the best relationship, but like, I know this is what's probably best for him."

I let out an emotionless laugh, one that just falls flat. But, Leyla can tell because she knows me. "I'm not upset over it." My voice cracks, I clear the lump in my throat reclaiming my confidence. "Does that make me a terrible person?" I don't waver, as I speak now. "I'm fucking eighteen years old, and the man's been nothing but cruel to me my entire life. I take care of him, even though he's so angry all the time and I just–" I clear my throat to conceal an unfamiliar emotion that clogs my throat. "I know that it's not his fault..."

Leyla cuts me off, "Cameron, you don't owe him anything anymore. You're doing something that will help him in the long run, and make your life easier." I can hear people in the background, even someone calling her name.

"Shit, you're busy. Sorry, I should have checked first before just slamming you with all of that." My guilt bubbles up, but Leyla doesn't let it simmer for any longer than it has to. She's always so in tune with me, she sees me without even being with me.

"Nope, you're fine, Cammy. I'm heading to Hazel's house now to work on some homework, but call me when you're done with your dad, okay? We can meet up at the park like old times. How does that sound?"

I can't help but smile. God she's just perfect in every way, shape, and form. "Yea, I'll call you after I get him settled, and we can go to the park."

I hang up with Leyla right as dad is coming out of the bathroom and mutter my way through explanations to convince him to come with me on a trip. Dad isn't phased by what's going on. He gets into the car without much fuss and just stares out straight ahead silently. My dad isn't old by any sense of the word, and this Dementia diagnosis was definitely something that I never saw coming. My dad was always so organized, so on top of everything. He was the one who constantly had everything planned to the 't' and never forgot a single thing.

Not anymore. He would have moments where he would remember everything and then moments like this, where he doesn't even remember he's awake and would stare off into the distance. I know taking him to this place would be the best option for him in my gut, and that needs to be enough for me.

———

Three hours later, my dad is settled into his new place. I walk out into the golden hour of sunlight and call Leyla; she answers on the first ring.

"You waitin' for my call, Ley?" I tease, the heaviness in my chest is pushed to the back, knowing that everything will be better. Leyla's laugh fills my soul, and I can't help but smile.

"No! I-I definitely wasn't." She lies through her teeth, and I laugh.

"Yea, yea. Anyway, I just finished up with my dad, that offer still on the table to meet at the park?" I startup my car and head towards that way anyway, knowing that even if she can't, I need to be not at my house right now.

"Yeah, of course. I can be there in ten minutes. I'll let my mom know I'm heading out." I can't help but smile, knowing that she's doing this for me. "See you soon. I'll meet by our tree."

———

I shouldn't be so excited—nervous? I don't know the right word but I feel *jittery*. But I shouldn't be, I'm only meeting up with Cameron. Yet, something about Cameron has never felt like *only* anything. He makes me jittery and yet calm all at the same time? He's special, not like anyone I've ever known, but also just him. I wish we could be more than just acquaintances, but I don't think he sees me that way.

I'm sitting at the base of the old oak tree that the old group used to hang out at after therapy on Saturdays for years. It's early May so the weather is still a little chilly, but I don't mind. I watch as the sun begins to set, casting a golden glow over the park.

"Hey you." A single crunch from old leaves that sit around us, the only evidence that seasons have passed. I jump as Cameron startles me, his footsteps so silent that I hadn't heard him coming.

"Cam! Jesus, you scared me!" I smile as I whip around to see him, my red hair bobbing around above my shoulders. I had this stupid idea of letting Hazel cut my hair because she saw it in a magazine.

"Sorry! I didn't mean to," Cameron smiles at me, butterflies take flight in my stomach, but I tamp it down cause we're just acquaintances. "I like the hair; it looks nice on you." Cameron's smile doesn't quite reach his eyes, the sparkle that I so often saw is dim– barely present.

The pain on his face tugs at my heartstrings, knowing that he is so clearly hurting, while acting like there is nothing going on. He is a good person, doing this for my benefit; as some sort of act of service to protect me, to not overload my plate. And yet, I see right through him.

I swish my hair with a smile, trying to distract him just a little. "Yea! Hazel cut it just now, I think it looks cute too!" My hand instinctively shoots out to grab his hand, pulling him down onto the ground with me so we can talk.

Cameron falls dramatically and lets out a forced laugh that leads into a bated silence. I want nothing more than to just make him feel better, his face looks so sad. A silence falls between us, not an awkward one, but one of simply being with someone you feel safe with.

"You okay?" I ask finally, breaking the silence and watch as the little divot between his brows remains unmoving.

"I-I'm okay." His voice cracks, betraying the brave face he's putting on. He looks so young, even with his black eye a myriad of greens and yellows. When I gently trace the bottom of the bruise with the pad of my thumb, he flinches away.

"Shit, sorry." I quickly pull my hand back, clasping my hands in between my legs.

"No, I'm sorry," he sighs. "I thought I'd be okay with getting my dad into the assisted living place. And like you know he's not really been the kindest to me, he's gotten so aggressive too. I know this is the best thing for him, but I can't help but feel guilty for going off to college and leaving him like this. Somewhere he doesn't know."

My hand grabs his and gives it a gentle squeeze, "You're human too, you know. With dreams of your own... You have to live your own life, and you're doing what's best for him. This is the right call." I smile reassuringly as I nod my head. He rubs the back of my hand with his thumb, and something inside me sighs happily. The way I want to just wrap him up and keep him safe is consuming, I don't understand why he of all people has to go through such pain.

"I wish it was just *easy*... I wish there was this distinct answer of what I should do—" His voice cracks at the end there, tears prick the corners of his eyes.

"I mean, I don't wanna leave my mom. She's done so much for me, but I mean I dream about going away to school in

Chicago with Hazel, and I get I'm still two years away but I know that there's something more out there, and you just can't let the present get in the way of your future."

His emerald eyes burn their way into my soul, as if he's consuming every word I say as a prayer. I put on a big smile and abruptly jump up and hold my hands out for him to take.

"Race you to the top?"

My eyes roving over the giant tree that we would hang out in for hours at a time. Knowing full well we are older, and climbing a tree isn't exactly *cool* anymore. A smile blooms on his face and I can't help but laugh as he jumps up and nods.

"You're on, Cherry Pie!" Cameron's face lights up, the way it used to when we were younger.

―――――

It is nearly 8PM when I check my phone and sigh before looking to Cameron.

"I don't want to leave, but I've gotta head home. You've always got my number, you know I'll always be here. Cause that's what friends are for."

The two of us had climbed up the tree and spent what seemed like an eternity just sitting and talking. I hope we can find time to spend like this, even when he's away at college, and I'm still stuck here. Even when I go off to Chicago for school— I mean, if Hazel and I get in. I want nothing more than to just escape this town with all the memories that exist here. Cameron's not going far for school, just a couple hours south in Detroit.

I think it just hit me that I'm gonna miss him when he leaves. I stop and turn around to him, his body just a shadow in the dark.

"Don't forget me, Cameron Curtis." I walk away before he replies.

4
CLIT MASTER 8000
LEYLA — 24, PRESENT DAY

This time of year is always really hard for me.

Family sits heavily in my mind as I take a sip of my iced chai at the little coffee shop on the corner. October is in full swing, and the leaves are a myriad of reds, yellows, and browns. The bustling town of Maplewood, nestled in the heart of Northern Michigan, is where I now reside. *Again.* I'm in my final year of school, and after what was a spectacular meltdown, I decided a reset was what I needed.

Things are getting difficult again. Although they haven't found the person responsible for my parent's death, Detective Alexandra, someone whom I have become rather close to throughout my life, called me the other day. She told me that they had received a new lead that may help the investigation. Hazel had told me to stay away, from Detective Alex, but I know staying in Chicago was only gonna go poorly for me. Home is calling, and that's where I am.

I know three things for certain:

1. I am still physically alone.

2. I have one person in my life who would be there for me no matter what.

3. This town is my last chance to make sense of my past, and my last chance to really figure out who I am.

Each corner holds a memory that could bring me to my knees. I sit in this little coffee shop, just as I had every single day since returning home. There is that one part of me that I know there's something calling to me here. I don't know what it is yet.

Hazel, my absolute best friend, and I are on our daily phone call, where she fills me in on all the gossip I am now missing out on. I could practically hear her rolling her eyes, trying her best to be excited about literally anything.

"Haze, I'm gonna need more than just 'they were talking'," I laugh softly. My face relaxes as I hear my best friend's laugh echo mine. I needed this. Hazel is the one person who makes the insanity that is my life feel like it has an ounce of normalcy.

"Do you want me to tell you that Denise and Eric fucked in the locker room while her brother, who we know is Eric's best friend, was in the shower in the next room over? He walked in and fully saw his best friend balls deep in his sister? Because that happened."

I spit out my tea, completely shocked by the words that spill from Hazel's mouth. "I'm sorry, *what?!* Girl, you've been holding out on me!"

Hazel's soft laugh fills a hole that has been slowly taking shape in my chest since leaving Chicago, a silence that has grown from the distance between us. Leaving Chicago wasn't something that I ever thought I was going to do, but as much as I thought it would be my freedom, it just wasn't. There is a part of me that was missing.

Hazel has always been the person who knows me better than anyone else in the world; my best friend, my other half. We are inseparable and I rely on her constant presence more than I care to admit. We met in group therapy when I was ten, and we've been inseparable ever since. We were practically raised together, and she was with me for what I considered the most formative years of my life.

I let out a sigh, briefly mourning my old life. Hazel had convinced me, after an argument that I let go on far too long, to move back to Maplewood, and give myself a chance to get some answers to questions that I am and have been too afraid to know.

"LeyLey? Are you doing okay?" I can hear the evident concern in Hazel's voice. I fall silent for a moment, unsure how to even start that conversation.

"I-I'm managing," I finally stammer out. I know I can't lie to my best friend, but right now, this is the best I can do. This is all that's left inside my broken soul.

"Say the word, Ley, and you know I'm just a flight away. I mean, we're almost finished here; we have a year left." Hazel paused. "Please, I mean it, Ley. You'd tell me if something was wrong?"

"Obviously. Listen, if I'm being honest, I think I need some me time with my Clit-Master 8000 and I'll be good as new." I hesitate, then sigh, anxiety rushing through me for no reason. I tell myself it's because I just mentioned my favorite sex toy in a quaint coffeeshop. "Haze, I'm gonna let you go, but... same time tomorrow?"

The tone of my voice is so desperate for this constant in my life. With how I feel that everything is crumbling around me, I'm pretty positive that if she doesn't call me tomorrow, I'll most certainly have some sort of panic attack.

"Of course. Love you, Ley."

"Love you, too." I end the call and put my phone away, standing up to order my third tea of the day.

———

I know I have to get this essay finished. Grabbing my cup, I put my headphones back on, blasting Ethel Cain, and melt away into my own little world. Hours pass and the sun begins to set. I type away on my laptop, my one-track mind knowing I will have to call it quits soon, but I keep going.

I'm just a tad too deep in thought when I think I hear something; a whisper of a sound that doesn't fully register but I look up from my laptop. When I finally pull my gaze from the screen, my face pales. On the table, sitting in front of me, is a single red rose.

"Hey, Callie?" I call out, looking at the woman who is

working at the counter. "Did you see where this would have come from?"

I bite my lower lip nervously while picking at loose skin on my nails as I look at the barista. She shakes her head and shrugs, "No, sorry, girlie pop. I didn't see anyone else in here but us. And you know I love you, but that ain't from me. Looks like you got a secret admirer. I'm so jealous, hah!" Callie continues her duties, unaware of the total tailspin I've initiated.

My heart races. This isn't the first time that this has happened to me. It happens *every year* around the anniversary of my parents' passing. These red roses randomly appear, no matter where I am or what I'm doing, and no one ever seems to know where they're coming from. I pack up my backpack making sure I grab everything as quickly as I can, I need to get out of here.

I run out the door to look around, desperately seeking any sort of strange figure that would finally put an end to this creepy mystery that plagues me every fall. Down the street there is a tall figure walking east, but they're so far down it couldn't be them. Then again, I don't really know when they dropped off the rose...

I'm sure it's nothing to worry about, it's *just* a flower, it's harmless. If I keep telling myself this, maybe only the thorns can hurt me this time.

5
ONE MORE TIME
LEYLA

A Few Days Later

I've been sitting in the local diner counter for at least an hour or two working on my essay before I'm distracted by the notification banner at the top of my phone's screen. My stomach flips in nauseating somersaults and my pulse quickens for several beats.

Shit. There is no reason I should be so upset over seeing that notification. Yet, the hairs on the back of my neck stand up, reminding me how just three days ago, I had mentioned needing to give this same person a call.

One Missed Call - Detective Alexandra

This is the last thing I need right now. The detective working on my family's murder case had taken a liking to me all those years ago and constantly tries to keep in touch beyond the scope of their cold case. And that's in spite of my best efforts to assure her that I am doing just fine on my own and absolutely do not need a babysitter. Afterall, I'm twenty-four now. But that hasn't deterred the persistent detective from checking in at least once or twice a month. Though, I suppose lately things have dwindled down. I haven't actually heard from her in a while, and I wonder if I'm not annoyed at the call, but at the absence of them lately. She's not Hazel, but she is another semblance of normalcy in my distorted life.

Honestly, she has done so much for me growing up that I really do owe her more than just a couple of phone calls a month. Alexandra is like a second mom to me she's the person who always checks in, makes sure I'm doing okay. I guess I don't realize all the things she's truly done for me and I really need to be better about keeping in touch with her. Just, not right now. Not today.

If I was smart, I would've told her about the roses and gifts I've been receiving. But, it's harmless. No one's ever done anything about it anyway.

I put my phone to the side after clearing away the call notification and turn my focus back to my computer, pulling up the syllabus for my Criminal Psychology class to double-check the due date. I groan inwardly at the sight. It's likely that I won't meet the deadline for my thesis, but I am lucky that my professors are understanding.

Even though I desperately tried to keep it to myself, it was only so long that I could hold it in and pretend like life is normal. So, my professors know about the police possibly finding my parents' killer and are more than willing to give me extra time.

Typing away on my computer, I am in a daze when the petite waitress, who looks like the crypt keeper's wife, startles me out of my stupor. "Anything else I can get ya, dear?" Her pronounced Midwestern accent drips over every word. Her rosy cheeks are bright and she chuckles as I nearly fall off of the chair from the suddenness of her appearance.

Once I calm my panicking heart, I plaster a sweet smile on my face and nod. "Yeah, I'll take another Coke..." I speak softly, almost to the point it would've been missed if someone wasn't paying attention. "Actually, I'll take an order of french fries too." I hadn't realized how long I have really been sitting here and don't want to come across as wasting the poor waitress' time. She jots it down and walks off.

My phone buzzes on the Formica countertop and lights up with another notification.

Det. Alexandra: *Hey Kiddo, just checking in. Haven't heard from you in a few weeks. I know the last time we talked I gave you some news that you didn't like. Wanted to make sure you're getting along fine in town and that no one's giving you any issues. OR ELSE!... Kidding! Ha ha. Sorry, my kids say I shouldn't use this—voice to text—well anyway. You have my number, Leyla, please reach out if you need anything. Have a good day!*

    Det. Alexandra: *Oh! Before I forget, I wanted to ask a small favor from you kiddo! I'm trying to start up a small program, kinda* *like you used to go to as a kid. I'm being promoted to Director of Program Outreach here in town, and I know you really benefited from something like that, and the ceremony is later today. I know it's last minute, but it's at Lebauer Park at 5! I'd love it if you would be interested in helping out with it! Let me know if you can make it, and if you'd want to volunteer with the start up! Talk soon!*

A rush of pain runs through my chest as I read the message over and over again, my heart clenching. Just another stark reminder of how alone in all of this wild world I truly am. A burning begins to form in the back of my eyes that I push against, not wanting to fall apart in public.

The waitress returns, placing my pop on the counter. "There ya go, sweetie! One pop for ya! Fries will be out shortly." A curt nod from me sends her bustling off. I adjust my hair in my ponytail, turning back to my laptop and typing away. I'll handle reality later; all that matters right now is getting this stupid paper finished.

———

After several hours working away at the diner, I pack up my belongings and throw my backpack on. I wave goodbye to the waitress, named Winnie, which I had discovered through no want of my own. I'm a little exasperated after she'd decided to tell me her entire life's story with her sixty-eight grandchildren. But honestly, as much as it annoyed me... A little distraction had been nice, as well as a little human interaction. Even if I didn't get more than a couple of words in here and there.

The weather is abnormally warm for mid-October in Upstate Michigan. A cool wind blows as I walk towards my new apartment, sending a chill through my entire body. There is just something off about this week; gooseflesh blossoms over my skin, and I feel an unsettling sensation that someone is watching me, that I am not alone. I spin around quickly, the ever-present feeling gnawing at me.

No one.

It is just me.

I think about it all, I think of what has happened in my life and I can't help but think maybe it would be a good idea to meet up with Alex, that maybe this ceremony for her outreach group would be a great place for me to start figuring out who I am again. I lost myself somewhere here in Maplewood, and I'll try anything to find *me* again.

I pull out my phone and send off a quick text that I'll be there to Detective Alex, and head home to change and clean up a bit.

With everything that has happened in the past few months, I can't help it; I am constantly on edge. I roll my eyes as I spin back around and keep walking down Lake Street. As I walk, every single thing that has happened these past few months flashes before my eyes, enough to knock the breath from me and leave my head spinning.

Get it together, Bitch, I chide myself. My fists clench at my sides as I look around, realizing that there isn't a single person in a two-block radius. I have no clue what is happening, but I've had enough of this feeling. I pluck my headphones out of my ears, quickly place them in my backpack, and hurry off to my apartment at an even brisker pace.

———

Couple hours pass and I'm sitting in a rideshare heading towards Lebauer for the ceremony. The park itself is crowded—definitely more crowded than I thought it would be. A sense of pride swells in my chest, knowing that the detective is going to be heading such an incredible program. The mayor calls her up, and gives a really fantastic speech about how incredible she has been for the community.

A single tear falls down my cheek as I see her walking up across the little makeshift stage that they've erected for this occasion. As the ceremony goes on, it's so clear how this entire town loves her, and how much she's truly done for this place. A niggle of guilt seeps in knowing that I haven't kept in contact with her as much as I should have. Detective Alexandra is given the floor, and my breath catches in my throat.

"Thank you!" she calls out. "Thank you all. This is such an incredible honor. I'm so touched to be given this amazing opportunity. I, myself, come from this small little town. I have been witness to so many unspeakable things being a detective. I've seen families destroyed, and new paths and journeys created from the embers of heartbreak. I have seen how these group outreaches have been so beneficial in creating fine, upstanding people. And I cannot wait to see what this new path brings, opening up opportunities and so many new doors for those who need it. It's truly an honor, and I promise I will not let you down in making this world a better place."

———

Detective Alexandra's speech comes to a close, and the crowd erupts into a round of applause, whistles, and yelps. The guilt wiggles its way back into my chest, and while I had the idea to head to say hi to Detective Alex, who am I to think she'd have time for me right now?

I make the decision to head home instead, as it's starting to get dark. I turn around back and pull out my phone, tapping out a little message to the detective. As I turn around, I suddenly crash into an out-of-thin-air brick wall. My body begins to fall backward, but a large, warm hand circles my wrist, pulling me up before I even hit the ground. It isn't a brick wall; it is a man. Not just any man, he is the most gorgeous man I've ever seen in my entire life. *Maybe there is someone looking out for me from up above.*

Realizing that the ground is no longer coming up towards me, his hand moves from my wrist and lands on my arm. He helps stabilize my balance as he smiles brightly. "Woah there!" he says with a chuckle.

I, however, am horrifically embarrassed and wish I had fallen, transformed into a worm, and sank into the ground to avoid this discomfiture. My eyes connect with his and I shake my head and bite my lower lip. "I am *so* sorry! I didn't mean to– I was distracted, and I was–"

There's a flip of my stomach; hairs stand up on the back of my neck. My intuition has been triggered like an alarm. Something about this moment doesn't feel real to me, this entire interaction seems off. Apparently, all of this must read across my face as he tilts his head in a movement that reminds me of a puppy.

"It's fine. Are you okay? You look like you've seen a ghost," the man asks, concern all over his face.

"Oh shit, yea, I'm fine. I'm so sorry for totally slamming into you. I've had an interesting day, and I just wasn't paying attention." I run my hand through my hair, my brow furrows as recognition hits me, I know him. Swallowing as a whisper of boldness hits me. My curiosity really can get the best of me sometimes. I can't help it, it's *gnawing* at me. "I'm sorry, I've gotta ask... Have we met before?"

The man looks at me like I grew a third head, but that friendly smile that is on his face shifts to a knowing smirk. "The name's Cameron. Cameron Curtis. And yes, Leyla, we've definitely met before."

My eyes open wide, instantly choking on my own saliva as I realize who this is in front of me. This Adonis of a man, this man who could be a statue in a museum, is the awkward, dorky, kid from group therapy when I was a kid. I am not sure why this is hitting me the way it is, and I definitely am not expecting heat in my stomach to pool when I look at him.

Cameron fucking Curtis is standing in front of me, in my hometown when last I heard he had moved to Detroit, and I have run into him like a fool. And now I'm standing in front of him, mouth gaping open as he studies me with a quirked brow.

Shaking my head I look at him, heat consuming my cheeks

from embarrassment, and I force a smile out and a host of unwelcome thoughts begin to permeate my brain.

I'm fine, I'm not in danger, no one will hurt me.

I haven't spoken to anyone from my group therapy days, besides Hazel, in *years* and especially not Cameron Curtis. I lost contact with him when he went away to college, and I never saw him as anything more than an acquaintance. A pang of a feeling I can't quite name hits me, my eyes facing the ground. But he definitely was someone who I spent a lot of time with. Realizing the awkward silence that hangs between us, I blink the stupor out of my head and force myself back to reality.

"O-Oh my god! Cammy! Hey– Hi! It's been such a long time! How are you?" A saccharine sweetness emanates from me as I push through the adrenaline that is inevitably going to be the death of me. The fire in Cameron's gaze doesn't go unnoticed, the heat in my own stomach needs to fuck right off or things are going to be bad, quick.

I really need to get laid, because there is absolutely no reason for there to be *butterflies flitting* around in my stomach right now. Fucking traitors.

"I'm good! It's nice to see you. What've you been up to? You look incredible." His voice rough, as Cameron runs his hand through his perfect dark blonde hair. *Damn*, he looks good.

How does one say barely alive, but making it through the days by the skin of my teeth? Right, we don't, cause that's my problem and not exactly small talk.

"I'm great. God, it's so good to see you." My smile softens ever so slightly, seeing the slight nerves on the man as he fidgets with his hands. "I have to ask, what are you doing here?

I mean what are you– why are...” I close my eyes for a moment as I shove the ever-present panic down.

“I go to the University. They’ve got an incredible psychology department. And, I was asked by Detective Alex to help out with her new program.” A smile is clear in his voice; it seems this sort of thing might be a passion for him. “I volunteer at the local Bigs and Littles program from time to time, and I thought this would be a great opportunity to help even more people than I already am.”

I’m thankful Cameron answers my jumbled question, saving me from embarrassing myself any more than I just did. *Why does that have me feeling some sort of way?* “What about you? What are you up to in good old Maplewood, Michigan? I thought you moved away for school?”

A small smile fights its way onto my face and it’s becoming more evident that despite myself, I’m not getting out of this conversation. “I go to the University, too!”

It hits me as we keep making small talk about school and the town. I feel comfortable around this man. Will it bite me in the ass? Probably.

As I’m about to make an excuse so that I don’t have to bother him any more than I already feel like I am, gentle hands land on both Cameron’s and my own shoulder. I subconsciously flinch back, and immediately find myself hoping that neither of them notices the stupid little movement. If they do notice, they don’t make note of it and so I ease a little.

Detective Alexandra’s powerful presence envelops us like a warm hug. It's as if time has stopped, I take in her beautiful, yet strong appearance, her cool dark umber skin tone glowing in the golden hour sun. I shake my head as I realize she's speaking to me.

"Huh? Oh, sorry." The practiced smile sits on my face and a blush creeps up my neck, reaching a fever point at the tip of my ears.

"I was saying what kismet that you two are here!

Just the two people I was hoping to run into today. Let me just say I am so glad you both made it today! So, as I started to tell you in my last message, Ley, I'm starting a new group-based outreach program, and I would love it if you two could get involved!" Her caramel eyes soften, as she looks at us expectantly and pats our shoulders.

I'm aware I should say yes— more than aware that I should *definitely* say yes to her. I look at Cameron whose easy demeanor is radiating off of him like a warm breeze.

He nods with a smile. "Well, I suppose I can go ahead and give you my official reply: I would love to help out. I think it would be a fantastic opportunity."

Alex claps her hands together excitedly with a smile, she turns to me, her blinding white teeth flashing my way. *Oh god, she wants my answer now too.* Pressure builds in my chest, but I try to breathe in the easygoing aura that comes from Cameron. Maybe if I could just borrow an ounce of it, I can get through the rest of this event without losing my mind from anxiety."Uh yea, sure. I guess that would be a cool thing to help out with." I say almost reluctantly, a smile as she grins even wider.

"Great! Thats–" Her voice is cut off and her head swivels as she's pulled away in another direction, that she just takes in stride. "Okay kids, I'll be in touch. And thanks so much– sorry– yes! I'm coming!"

And as quickly as she was here, she's gone. Cameron lets out a huffed laugh as he watches Detective Alex's figure being ushered off to talk to a small gaggle of press. Cameron and I stand there in the quiet awkward silence that shimmers around us. Even though I've been itching to get out of his hair this entire time in fear I'm somehow holding him up or being a bother, now that I'm looking at the lull in conversation where we could easily go our separate ways... I don't want to say goodbye.

I decide to take the leap, despite all the chaos in my life right now. I ask, smiling up at him, breaking the silence at last. "Wanna go for a drink?"

He nods emphatically, and smiles. "Would love to, Cherry."

My heart flutters at that nickname that he gave me so long ago, and for some reason I just know that tonight is going to be a good one.

6
OLD FRIENDS
CAMERON 26, PRESENT DAY

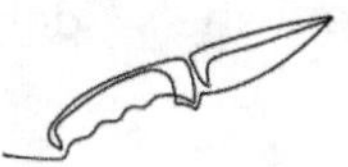

"So, how are you?" I ask with a grin on my face. My mind starts to wander as soon as she begins to tell me all the things she's been up to. Leyla could tell me anything and it wouldn't really matter. *I've never let her out of my sight.*

Since the moment I met her, she has been **mine**.

She doesn't know it yet, but Leyla Clarkson will belong to me— no matter what the cost. I look at this stunning woman in front of me, this goofy grin immovable on my face as we sit at Kris's Music Bar. It is a tiny dive, only the locals go here so most nights aren't crazy busy, and exactly the reason I decided this would be the best place to take her. It's somewhere we won't get interrupted. I need this to be perfect and want to spend time with her. *Only* her. No one else around, no huge groups of people, no Detective Alex.

I don't really believe in love or anything of the sort, but the way my chest constricts when I'm around Leyla is something out of one of those romance novels. I know that's not me, though. In my life, love always comes with a cost and it is usually held over my head.

Her laugh shocks me out of my swirling thoughts. Our eyes connect and my smile softens as I nod in agreement to whatever it is that she's saying. I realize, however, that this is probably my first mistake; she's definitely looking at me expectantly.

"You asked me a question that wasn't a yes or no answer, didn't you?" I truly can't tell based on Leyla's face what was going through her mind but I knew that I really needed to stop getting in my damn head around this girl.

"I did. I asked what have you been up to?" Leyla chuckles softly, somehow not a hint of judgement in her voice. My shoulders sag, releasing the tension that I didn't even know I had been holding, and I finally meet her gaze. Her unwavering smile leaves this warm feeling in my chest. I sigh deeply as I drink in the moment; I'm more content than I'd been in a long, long time.

I answer her with a breezy tone, "I've been awesome. Keeping busy with working part-time at the hospital nowadays. I was taking care of my dad for a bit, but he passed away last month." I look down as a lump forms in my throat.

Her face falls as she reacted to my words. I'm not sure if she remembers my upbringing, but when she replies, I'm reminded of how she has always been able to truly see me.

"I would say 'my condolences', but I would be lying. How are you holding up?"

Even without my twisted sense of loyalty and devotion, she's perfect for me. She's not afraid to speak her mind with me, and she cares. Leyla isn't just asking how I'm holding up to make conversation, I know that she's seeing me as someone more than just a face. She sees me.

Our conversation is interrupted by the waitress. She takes our orders, Leyla ordering a vodka cranberry, me, a whiskey ginger. When the waitress walks away, my eyes instantly connects with Leyla's again.

"I'm doing okay, it got hard towards the end. He had dementia so he would have these moments of just pure rage, which to everyone else was a symptom of the dementia. But, I knew him, he was–"

"Always that monster?" she answers for me, my heart seeming to come to a halt as I nod in agreement.

"It got worse as it progressed, but there were days of lucidity, where he would be that kind dad that I remembered when my mom was alive, ya know?" I drag my hand through my hair and take a deep breath. "He didn't even remember she was dead some days. He'd ask me when mom was going to come visit him, those days always were the hardest for me. 'Cause then I'd have to explain why she wasn't coming to visit. I would make excuses, but it got to a point where it would upset him so much... *too* much... I just started distracting him with other things so he wouldn't get agitated anymore." I sighed, my eyes widening as I looked at Leyla. "Oh my god, I'm sorry, Cherry. This is such a depressing conversation for our first time talking in, god, what– eight years?"

Eight years, four months, eleven days to be exact.

This beautiful fucking woman smiles at me. I watch as the blush creeps up her neck and it's as if there is nothing wrong in the world. There's just us in this crappy little bar that will no doubt become one of my fondest places to remember. My heart sings with the harmony and glee of a choir as I study every little detail of that gorgeous smile.

I will make her mine, no matter what it takes.

———

We sit in the bar for a couple hours, laughing and smiling without a care in the world. She takes a sip of her drink and giggles; her eyes piercing a hole into my psyche.

"You're incredible!" Leyla beams up at me after I tell some really cheesy joke. I watch as she fights some internal battle in the matter of milliseconds, but then she says something that utterly shocks me.

"Did you want to come over? To my place? Now?" The look in her eyes as she watches for my reaction sinks into me and I don't know if this is some sort of test or not. Honestly, I don't even care if it is, I am not going to miss out on this opportunity.

Because of my shock, I apparently took too long to answer. She stammers out again, "You don't have to— I mean— Oh my god, I'm sorry I totally read the vibe— I—"

"Let's go," I reply hastily, interrupting her panicked exclamation before quickly closing out our tab. I smile like a kid on their way to a candy shop. It seems tonight, something sweet is indeed in my future. Tonight, I am the luckiest man in the world.

"Lead the way." I hold out my arm as we step out of the bar, and we are running off towards her apartment.

7
MORE PLEASE
LEYLA

Honestly, I have no clue what I was even thinking. I never take men home; and I certainly never invite men back to my place after the first date. I mean we were acquaintances at best when I knew him, but I'm going to be bold tonight. Let's see where this goes. Plus, I'm feeling a little bit tipsy, and Hazel has been more than blunt about the fact that I need to loosen up a bit.

I fumble around in my purse trying to find my keys, my traitorous body betraying me as the blush creeps up my neck to my cheeks. I truly don't understand what is happening, but the look on Cameron's face makes goosebumps cover my arms.

"S-Sorry, stupid key," I say as I finally find the damn thing and get the door open. All I can think about is quickly ushering this gorgeous man into my apartment and *really* not wanting Mrs. Fitz in 2A screaming about impropriety happening in *her* hallway. "It's nothing to write home about, but it's mine, you know?"

I look around, realizing that I definitely should spend more time cleaning my apartment, but at this point, it's too late. I glance up at him, a touch embarrassed, but he doesn't seem to care, and if he doesn't then neither do I.

"Nice place. I didn't realize how close we live to each other. I'm two blocks over on Easton," Cameron smiles at me. I watch as he takes in the eclectic furniture that I have acquired over the years. Why nerves are hitting me right now, I have no idea, but I look at Cameron and grin sheepishly. His eyes flash something hidden and unknown to me.

I hear Hazel's voice in my head– she's squealing with excitement, telling me that I should get laid. Why not with someone who I definitely know is safe?

"Keep the night going? I think I have some whiskey here somewhere." I open all my cabinets and search for the whiskey, peering back briefly to gauge his response. Cameron, looking suave, leaning up against my counter, simply nods.

"Sure, sounds good to me. That is, if you're going to be joining me."

I smile— that damn blush is blooming once again on my cheeks, *just* as I calmed my overactive heart from nearly jumping out of my chest. I pour us both a glass of whiskey and then invite him to sit down on the couch; though I rush ahead to pick up the books that litter it, placing them neatly on my coffee table. I sit down next to him, I crane my head then turn my body to give him my full attention.

"So..."

"So..."

I bite my lip and look away. This unknown shyness hitting me is what an out of body experience feels like I bet. I'm not the least bit shy, at least not anymore, but there is something about him that makes me feel like this could be something fun. It isn't like me, but something is feeling right and I'm never one to give into these urges so early on.

How could I possibly be into the man whose father – *Don't go there Leyla*, the little voice in my head screams at me. Our eyes meet and I know that he is feeling the same way I am. This doesn't have to be anything more than a girl just needing sex. It doesn't have to be more than that— I *can't* want more than that.

We talk for what seems like hours, telling stories from the years that had separated us and joking about the days we had shared. The more moments that pass, the closer I inch. *Who said this has to be more than a one time thing*? I ask myself again.

Slowly, he leans in, and I meet him halfway. Our lips touch softly at first, almost like they are posing a question. I can feel the warmth coming off his body, his lips gentle against mine. There is nothing rushed about it. He is taking his time and I want to savor it too. Every second. Every breath. This is unexpected to say the least, but I'm over second guessing everything.

He pulls back and we sit in silence for a few moments, as I try to keep my breathing even. I keep stealing glances at him, his emerald eyes are focused on some point ahead, his jaw clenched like he's trying to keep himself in check. I can't blame him. My own heart is racing, my body still unsure of what to do next.

There had been moments when we were growing up when there were glances that lingered a little too long, and touches that felt almost too intimate for just friends. But this? This was different. When I finally meet his gaze, everything *shifts*. His eyes soften a little, as if he can read the uncertainty in mine. He leans in slightly, just enough to close the space between us, and my pulse quickens.

"I never thought we'd end up here," I whisper, my voice sounding smaller than I want it to.

Cameron exhales, the air between us thickening. Then, his lips part, his voice lowers to almost a murmur. "Trust me, it's something I've thought of before."

I nod, more to myself than to him, feeling a mixture of nerves and something else— something warm, something I no longer want to ignore. I can feel my body leaning toward him without even thinking about it. Everything inside me is telling me this is *the* moment. I'm ready.

I hadn't realized how much I wanted this until I was here, this close to him. But I am still holding back, unsure at my core. Cameron doesn't push. Instead, his hand finds mine, his fingers brushing against it gently, almost hesitantly. It's a soft touch, a question in the way he holds my hand. Am I ready? Is he?

I can feel his uncertainty, but I also feel his strength. The way he holds onto me isn't desperate— it's steady. Comforting. And that's how I know.

"Are you sure?" he asks, his voice barely above a whisper. His thumb gently traces the back of my hand.

I swallow, my throat dry, but I don't hesitate. "I'm sure," I say, my voice stronger than I expect. Slowly, he leans in, and I meet him halfway. Our lips touch again, soft at first. I can feel the warmth of him, his lips gentle against mine. There is nothing rushed about it. He is taking his time, giving me control, giving me the go ahead to continue. I relish the all-encompassing feeling of his tongue against mine. This is a moment I wish could last longer than just this second in time.

His hand slides from mine, to my waist and pulls me closer. I let myself fall into it, he deepens the kiss. Our breaths are interconnected, like we are both virgins, figuring this out for the first time. I could feel the beat of my heart in my chest, louder and faster the closer he gets to me. My fingers tangle in his hair, his other hand comes up to cup my cheek, and his touch sends a ripple of warmth through me.

When we finally pull back, breathless and flushed, my forehead rests against his. I close my eyes, my heart racing, trying to calm the storm inside me. I don't want to overthink this. I don't want to ruin it.

"Are you okay?" he asks, his voice tender; his one hand still resting on my face, thumb gently stroking my skin, the other still gripping my waist. I nod, opening my eyes just enough to look up at him. The air in the room has changed, it isn't soft and gentle anymore, it is passionate and heated.

"More than okay," I whisper breathlessly, smiling softly. Biting my lower lip, my hand traces up and down his defined biceps. I lean in and our lips crash together, hard, and rough. The fire that burns in my core pulses as I crawl up to him, my knee between his legs.

He angles himself towards me. A moan slips out of my mouth as I lick his lips, my tongue pressing forward demanding entrance. He opens for me, an indecent, guttural moan escaping from his lips as he returns the kiss.

"Cherry." The breathless word that leaves Cameron's mouth sends a shiver down my spine, leaving me feeling undone and we lose it.

In a sudden frenzy his hands are all over my body, exploring every inch of me, touching, grazing. Hard calluses rake along my back as he pulls my shirt off and onto the floor next to us. He takes me and leaves me panting as our eyes connect again. His head leans into my neck, hot breath hitting behind my ear as he nips at my pulse point, sending it fluttering through the roof. His teeth are pulling at my ear, my back arching reactively as a whimper escapes my lips.

"Cam–" I can't speak, as if all words have emptied from my mind as this man begins to worship my body like it's all he knows. Cameron pushes me back onto the couch, his hand gripping my bare waist as he peppers kisses down my collar bone, his body hovering.

"You're. Fucking. Stunning." Cameron's voice is confident and breathy somehow at the same time. He continues lower, his eyes burning a hole through my soul as he looks up at me through heavy lidded eyes. He's silently asking for permission one last time. I nod a little too aggressively as he slowly makes his way to my breasts, sucking the left nipple he begins to cup my right, my body feels as though it's on fire. Every nerve ending lights up along it.

"More—d" I somehow get out as he caresses both breasts

with fervor, looking up at me through hooded eyes. His once clear green eyes are dark with lust as my back once again arches in pleasure from just his mouth, he smirks at me.

"Tell me, Cherry, would you like me to worship you with my fingers or my tongue? Best choose quickly, because I need to know if you taste as sweet as you look," in a voice that wholly doesn't sound like him.

"Tongue– god yes– fuck..." The words escape my lips far too quickly to be casual. This man has my entire body reacting in ways I didn't even know possible. In a moment, my entire body wracked with want, as he forces my leggings down my legs around my ankles. The anticipation and pleasure intensifies as he rips away my underwear, his eyes dark when he looks up at me from in between my legs.

"God, Cherry– you're fucking dripping."

I tense up as his finger glides down my clit and a noise, I'm not even certain is human, leaves my mouth. Without warning, he thrusts his tongue into me. I grasp onto the couch, arching my back putting more pressure onto his tongue, as the pleasure radiates through my body. He curls his tongue in a way that coaxes me to my breaking point, and the heat mixed with plea-sure begins to build in my back.

"I-I... Cam– I'm–" I fight the words to come out, my head tilts back and my eyes catch on something red on my windowsill. A metaphorical bucket of cold water hits me as my eyes fly open and I'm pushing myself away from him.

"No, no, no..." I scoot backwards, falling off the couch as Cam sits there for a moment looking confused.

"Leyla– are you okay? What... What's wrong?" The concern

flickers in his eyes, as he sets himself right. He doesn't see it, the blood pulsing through my ears is no longer from my near orgasm moments before. It's from the utter terror of seeing the long-stemmed rose sitting outside on my windowsill. The air in the room feels like it's below zero and I can't fucking *breathe*. My hand flies up to my chest and immediately I'm grabbing for my shirt.

I'm having a fucking panic attack.

8

TIGHT CHEST, SOFT HANDS

CAMERON

My heart sinks as I watch Leyla begin to have a panic attack. I'm no stranger to them but it somehow doesn't make it any easier to know that there's nothing I can do to directly stop it.

"Leyla. Leyla, look at me. *Breathe.* You're okay, it's okay. What's going on?" I look at her, utterly confused.

I haven't the slightest clue as to what is going on with her or what caused her to go from riding my face one moment, to gasping for air the next. Her face is pale and she's muttering something over and over, about it not happening again. My gaze follows hers while she's mid-panic and that's when I see it. A single red rose on her windowsill.

"Cherry, look at me. Look at me, I'll get rid of it, okay? Just focus on breathing for me." I'm almost certain every word I've said has gone in one ear out the other. But, I'm running over to the window, flinging it open, grabbing the rose, and tossing it on her counter. My body instinctively pulls her close to me, I'm aware I'm essentially a stranger, but clearly my words aren't doing much for her.

Her body is vibrating with an unfettered fear, and I don't know how to help her. This is so out of my comfort zone, but I hold her and let her sob into my shirt. I look at that stupid rose sitting on her counter and I have no idea where this thing came from. I just know whoever it is, I will find them.

Minutes pass and it seems that her sobs have finally calmed down. I run my hand up and down her back and break the thick silence, "Ley?" Her tear-stained face runs through me as if it is a truck running a red light, but she lets out a soft sigh and clears her throat.

"I-I'm so sorry," Leyla stutters out as I run my hand through her hair, trying to calm her even further. Leyla's body shakes as the tremors of anxiety run through her.

"Cherry, please, I need you to breathe."

Her breaths are heavy and uneven, but when she looks away and not at me, my entire heart shatters.

"Ley," I grab her chin and force her to look at me. "Breathe in," she matches my breaths. "Eyes on me. Good. That's my good girl." My hand runs through her hair, as we continue to calm her breaths down.

Leyla attempts to pull away, and starts mumbling something about being fine, and some other bullshit excuse, but I'm not having any of it.

"Nope!" I pop the *'p'* in the word dramatically, trying to distract her. "None of that," I say as I gently push her away from my body so I can look at her directly. "You ready to talk about what the hell is going on? 'Cause a reaction like that doesn't just happen from a one-time occurrence."

Leyla purses her lips and rolls her neck before she looks at me. "I've gotten them every year since my parents were killed." Her face is pale when she looks at me, little tremors running through her hands. "This is the second one this week, and I just... I can handle one, and it's just that it's normally in public you know? This is at my home– my–"

"Your safe place, I get it." I sit back on the couch as she keeps her head down, not really making eye contact with me while she stays sitting on the floor.

"Exactly. I-I'm still really sorry. I bet this wasn't how you expected tonight to go." Leyla is still shaking as she speaks. I wrap my arms around her as I shake my head.

"I had no expectations, Cherry. This was just two friends catching up. My only concern right now is making sure you can breathe." My arms instinctively tighten around her and I'm more than happy to just sit here with her while she comes down from her panic attack. "How about this: I will make you some tea, you seem like the type of girl who likes tea, and we can just sit here and watch a movie okay?"

The slightest nod from her has me gently letting go of her and helping her up to the couch before I walk into her kitchen, fill the tea kettle, and pull a mug from her cabinets. Minutes later, a steaming cup of tea is in her hands, I've grabbed the remote from the coffee table, and I'm sitting back down on the couch. I'm just far enough away to give her personal space, but in a moment she's scooting this way and leaning against me as I wrap my arms around her.

"Is this okay?" Her voice is honestly too quiet for my own liking, and it makes my blood boil that someone is out there harassing *my* Leyla, leaving her in such a state.

"Cherry, listen to me, okay? All of this? It's not okay that it's happening to you, and in no way is it okay that it's bothering you so bad." I gently give her another little squeeze. "I am here as someone for you. I am more than okay with you laying up against me. I want you to be comfortable. I want you to know that I'm your friend, and you are safe."

I visibly watch her as her shoulders fall, the tension releasing as she lays her body against mine. She lets out a deep breath and we watch a movie. Her hair falling over her shoulder, her eyes wet with emotion, pink sitting on her cheeks. She looks so fucking small in this moment, she looks like she could just keep falling apart, her body vibrates with unspent adrenaline.

9

DEAD WEIGHT

THE WHISPERING KILLER

avid West, 52, 4 Women Murdered.

I pull out the folder from its' hiding spot in the hole in the wall, along with all of the other files on my list. This is always my favorite part. I've spent the last couple of days getting as much information on him as I could: locations, evidence, confessions, anything I possibly can to give the family of his victims a bit of closure. Just one word that could make the already horrific event they're living any easier. Letting the families and friends at least know they no longer have to live in fear, or wonder if they themselves are next.

I have no regrets. Not one.

As I flick the light switch on, the hum of the lights and its dim radiance fills the room. The man sitting in the middle of the room whimpers through his cloth gag; one that I've not bothered to change since I stuffed it into his mouth over seventy-two hours ago. I put the file down on my desk. My attention is set on the sack of shit sitting in my basement, tied up and gagged. A tight laugh escapes my lips as a thought occurs to me; *I really need to see my therapist.* In these situations, I feel nothing good. Only an ever-present rage that simmers through my body.

"What's that? You're just *so* excited to see me?" I growl to the perverted monster sitting in the chair, his face barely recognizable at this point. I'm shocked that the man is still alive. A wicked smile grows on my face as I roll out my tools needed for the next bit of torture that I'm set to deal to him. My fingers dance over the surgical, clean instruments, biting my lower lip as I smirk towards David.

"Oh, darling David. I feel as though we've grown so close these past few days, don't you? You make what I have to do next, so much harder!" The lie rolls off my tongue in a saccharine sweet lullaby.

The knife in my hand reflects the light and David flinches back. He screams and thrashes as the smell of urine reaches my nose. I walk towards the man, and the sweet sounds of what I can only assume are pleas for his life fill the space. I adjust my balaclava as I start the video camera and circle David like a lion going in for their kill.

"How pathetic. Just like the pathetic waste of life you are," I hiss his direction, modulating my voice for the stream, as the knife in my hand points towards his cock. I waste no time pushing it down, just hard enough to hear the ripping of his filth ridden pants.

I grin as the adrenaline flows through my body, I roll my shoulders and head to crack my joints, my eyes connecting with

David's. His body thrashes with what little energy he has left, which truly isn't much after three days of torture. I lean down and remove the man's pants with my gloved hands, and grin towards the camera. Which, luckily, doesn't show below the man's waist.

"David West here decided he was going to rape and kill four women, for fun. We know we can't have that, now, can we?!" I turn away from David, a smile hides beneath my mask as I turn back to his shivering body. With one swift motion I press the knife into the man's cock again and slice it off. Blood begins spurting as his cock rolls to the floor. David's anguished screams echo through the basement. I grin as he cries out in utter pain.

I lift my knife, hold it to his neck, and slash quickly. There's no fight left in him. A gurgle escapes as David struggles to breathe before finally falling silent. The light in his eyes fades into a vacant stare that burrows into the darkness surrounding us. David's body goes limp, and the distant sound of blood dripping slows, telling me that he's dead. I revel in the silence, savoring the thrill of my kill.

I turn to the camera, an unnatural tilt of my head as I walk towards it. Silence echoing all around us as I turn off the recording and begin my clean up. This is quick, this is the easy part. I have no guilt as I begin to hose off the mess. I tell myself that guilt only makes me weak— and I am not that. David West is dead, and I am the one who did it.

I put on some loud rock music as I wrap up his body and get him prepped for transport.

One down. Millions more to go.

10

THE CLEAN UP

LEYLA

How fucking embarrassing. I invite a man—an old friend at that— over to my house, and not only do I let him eat me out, but mid-almost-orgasm: I have a panic attack. I stayed in his arms for a ridiculous amount of time as he comforted me. Cameron listened to every single word I said and not an ounce of judgement came from him. I look down at my phone seeing that he has texted me, four times now, and I have yet to reply.

The idea that he held me through my panic attack, let me remember how to breathe, pass out while watching a movie, then carried me to my room, meant more to me than one could ever fucking begin to explain. I woke up to a bottle of water, some Tylenol, and his number scribbled onto a Post-It is sitting on my counter.

There's something mortifying about the fact that I was so open to this man I hadn't seen in nearly eight years that has me reeling. Even just thinking of him made me realize a part of me that I thought was closed off, has somehow started to crack open and let me see that there is still good in the world.

"I should text him."

I work on braiding my hair as I look at my video call with Hazel, who is sitting at her vanity putting on makeup for some date she was going on. Hazel's jaw dropped as she turned and looked at me.

"Leyley, that's what I'm telling you. This man talked you through an entire panic attack and did all that cute shit for you, and you mean to tell me that you're ghosting him?"

"...Yes. I am doing exactly that."

I look at Hazel incredulously, her face matching mine. I let a small smile take over my lips as I look at her. "Okay, okay. I'll text him and see about having dinner." I pull my phone off of the desk and pull up Cameron's text thread. "Haze, what do I even say? Hey bud, thanks for giving me the best blue balls ever, wanna try again? Or, or I know! Thanks for tongue fucking me and then holding me while I have a panic attack then promptly fall asleep on you after? This dude is too good for me, and I already know that."

"Babes, you can just say hey. He clearly likes you if he's been checking in on you."

There is a long pause filled only with my mild annoyance. "I hate that you're always fucking right," I finally mutter. I quickly tap out a little message to Cameron and put my phone back on the charger, hoping that in between waiting for him to reply and me putting it there, my phone will spontaneously combust. That way I can just keep living in my safe little bubble, away from others. Even Cameron. He's too good for me, and I don't want to get *anyone* involved in the shipwreck of my life.

Not even a moment later, my phone buzzes and an unintentional squeal escapes my lips as I see the notification pop up across the top of the screen. "He responded," I blurt out as Hazel continues her talking.

> Cameron: Hey 😉
>
> Cameron: I'm working right now, but I'm off at 5 if you wanna do something? I've got just the thing.

"Shit!" I run over and pick up the phone. "Sorry Haze, freaked out a bit there." I laugh awkwardly as I look at the text thread and then back to the video call.

"Leyley! The fuck did he say?! You can't leave me hanging like that!" Hazel's overly enthusiastic voice echoes through the room. I hesitate, a noise coming from the back of her throat as Hazel interrupts again. "LEYLA JOY CLARKSON!" Hazel teases once again, full naming me; I can't help but bite my lip with a smirk.

"Oh my god, you're insane." I tease, but then relent. "He asked to go to dinner tonight... I should say–"

"You should say yes, and I will take it as a personal offense if you don't," Hazel huffs. I sit here, truly not sure if she's joking or not.

She's not.

"Fine, *fine*. I'll say yes." I begrudgingly agree, then look at the time. "I've gotta let you go, Haze. I'll text you tonight."

"Please don't, because girl, if you're not finally getting that sweet sweet cock that we *know* you need, I will come to Michigan and slap you."

"Haz– that bitch hung up," I mutter to her, then to myself.

An unsettling sense of relief hits me, I'm slightly relieved that she hung up on me. I love talking to Hazel, and I normally have no issues blabbing every detail of my life to her, but for some reason, with everything I've been doing I feel almost guilty telling her. Detective Alex has been a sensitive subject with her lately, and if I were to tell her that we are talking again, and that I'll be helping out with her new group... I worry that Hazel would feel betrayed.

That twinge of guilt hits me as my decision to rejoin the group sends an unsettling pain through me. Closing my eyes, I try to think back to those years ago when that was me in the group, I try to think back to my younger years and I'm met with this heavy fog that's sat there for so fucking long. Cameron's presence is a gentle distraction that things can still turn out okay.

Leyla: Sure, where?

Cameron: I'll pick you up.

Leyla: See you soon!

————

An hour passes and I've somehow fully gotten ready, hair curled and flowing down my back in loose ringlets. I've got a long-sleeved black crop top on, with light wash boyfriend jeans. I toss on my white sneakers and look at myself in the mirror. *What the fuck am I doing?* I question, but in that quick moment, I realize I'm more than okay with this. I look cute, I deserve to have fun, and I deserve to go out with an old friend.

An old friend whose face I have now sat on.

I check my phone for the time and my body warms when I see a message from Cameron that he's on the way. I start sharing my location with Hazel– can't trust anyone these days. Even an old friend. Right, I'm going to get outside and wait before I talk myself out of this and hide in bed.

Forcing myself to move, I grab my purse and keys before moving to stand out by the lamppost. I put my back to the cold metal, finding a strange comfort in the jarring sensation. Maybe because it gets me out of my head, or maybe because my anxiety has me running a little warmer than usual.

Suddenly, I feel my hair stand up on the back of my neck. That sensation of not being alone is weighing down the air around me. *No,* I can't let this feeling ruin my night. There is no one out to get me, I'm just being paranoid.

I look down at my phone to keep distracting myself. When a car honks, I jump, but then a smile grows on my face. It's an older Maserati, black and you can tell that it's definitely well taken care of. "Cam! Hey!" I smile as he gets out of the car and opens the passenger side door for me.

"Madam," Cam says playfully, as he bows dramatically and motions for me to get into his car.

"Oh my, what a gentleman," I say as I get in, his warm suede scent envelops me, a beaming smile on my face. All sense of nervousness just vanishes from my body in the presence of Cameron Curtis. How *dangerous*.

"So, do I get any hint of what we're doing tonight for 'dinner'?" I ask in air quotes with a quirked brow on my face all the while secretly loving the fact that I haven't the slightest clue what we're doing. I've gladly handed him the metaphorical keys to let him drive the evening. My brain could use a break, even if the Type A side of me is screaming in the trunk.

"It's a surprise, but I promise you'll love it."

Cam smiles at me, a slight dimple on his right cheek makes an appearance. It's admirable to be so confident in himself when he knows so little about me. And somehow, it adds to the thrill of it all for me, as I can't wait to tease him about how wrong he is. People often make assumptions about me and my interests, and they are never right.

Patiently, I watch as he drives us to this mystery location. I try to guess and toss out random places and things, but everything is shot down. I glance over at Cameron, he looks so confident, so casual. It's completely entrancing. I can't take my eyes off of him.

"We're almost there, Cherry," He says as his eyes connect with mine for a fraction of a second. I'm staring at him, probably looking like some infatuated fool, when really I'm just trying to figure out where the hell he's taking me. I laugh awkwardly and nod.

"Yea, yea, okay." I scrunch my nose, internally admitting defeat and then turn to look out the window at the town that I want to feel like home again. It's not until we turn down the street that the giant screen comes into view, with a line of cars that are all heading into the same spot. "The drive-in?!" I exclaim, almost too excitedly as he looks at my overjoyed expression.

"I take it this was a good choice?" Cameron smirks at me. He turns away as the car rolls to a stop at the ticket booth, he pays for the two of us. When he turns back to me, the light in my eyes is bright and I smile, nodding excitedly.

"I've always wanted to go to a drive-in," I admit, a little bashfully. I feel my cheeks starting to hurt from how big I'm smiling. "I've never been to a drive-in. Good guess, Cam."

"Well, I will happily pop your drive-in movie cherry, Cherry. I promise you this will be the best first time experience you've ever had." Cameron pulls into a parking spot, the gravel crunching beneath the tires as he slides the car to a stop.

The light from the gigantic movie screen in front of us flashes with colorful pictures and ads, and I feel something foreign to me building up in my chest, bubbling up just beneath the surface even more as he puts the top down of the classic Maserati, and the crisp autumn air hits me. My gaze shifts to find Cameron sitting there, looking just like he always does— too casual, with an odd grin on his face. It's as if he has some kind of secret that he's not telling me.

I shrug it off, but I can't help feeling that there might be something more to it, maybe even to us. Something... deeper. I can't quite place it. Maybe it's the years that passed, or the fact that we both grew up, but I can tell we're not just 'two old friends' catching up anymore.

The title of the movie is written with letters on a marquee, *The Lost Boys* with the second 'O' definitely being a zero. I laugh at the absolute cheese of this entire encounter but take a breath realizing that my chest has a weight off of it for the first time in a while; somehow, this only happens when I'm around him lately. I take in everyone around us, the ambience of the drive-in, and my cheeks start to ache from all the grinning.

"Okay, I've got blankets in my trunk. I snuck in some snacks, and I can run and grab us some hot dogs or burgers from the concession stand," Cam says as he opens his door and moves to the back of the car. Popping the trunk, he pulls out two cozy blankets, a pack of Twizzlers, and some M&M's. I start to get out of the car to help him grab everything, but Cam slams the trunk shut and quickly makes his way back to me.

I tuck a loose strand of hair behind my ear as I lean against his car. "I could go for a burger, I'm starving." Standing this close to him, I can't help but tilt my head, really looking him over. He's tall and I'm not exactly short, but he has to be at least six feet tall, and my mind wanders to a place that definitely isn't appropriate for a drive-in.

Cam's face darkens ever so slightly as he looks at me, and I'm dying to know what is going on his mind. "Burgers it is. Let's go."

It's a quick trip to the little building set back from the cars with picnic tables that look as old as the drive-in itself and a thick smog of delicious grease promising us an artery-clogging delight. Before long, we are back at his car with the paper bag and Styrofoam cups between us.

"Ready, Leyla?" he asks radiantly as we are officially settled in for the movie.

This feeling in my chest is somehow light and effervescent,

completely at odds with the usual numbness I'm accustomed to. I don't know what it is, but being around him makes me feel safe, complete. I read all those romance novels and judge them so harshly knowing that shit like this is a fairytale, a good story for naive girls who have never had anything bad happen to them.

People don't get second chances. This doesn't just happen, especially not to people like me. I turn to Cam and his face is furrowed, but when he notices me looking at him, a smile blooms on his face.

The movie begins, the sounds of it crackling through the ancient speakers makes the back of my head tingle. We don't talk much at first— just sit watching the stupid plot unfold and laughing at the over-the-top drama. I'm comfortable around Cameron in a way that I have really only ever felt with Hazel. I clear my throat softly enough that it doesn't interrupt the others, Cam turns to me with his kind eyes, causing a shiver to run through my body.

"So, I guess I should thank you for the other night," I finally work up the courage to say. "I really am sorry for disappearing on you for a few days. I won't lie, I was pretty shocked you responded."

I catch a flash of a frown on his face and he gently reaches his hand out to me, our fingers interlacing with each other's. "Leyla, a little panic attack is not going to scare me away that easily. You know what kind of life I grew up with. I promise you, I know how to handle a panic attack. Honestly, it kills me that you're even going through this. I'm here, okay? For whatever you need."

I'm fairly certain I feel my ovaries put on war paint, kick into overdrive, and signaling every alarm. He's something they — and I— have always wanted to hear. So they're screaming at me to keep this man forever and make little Camerons run all over the place. I truly can't believe that this is something that is happening to me. How is it that this boy from my childhood is turning out to be literally the most perfect man?

"It really means a lot to me." I shove him playfully moments after the words leave my lips, as if I can't let the moment sit in sincerity too long or else he will catch a glimpse of something I'm afraid to show. He catches my hand and plants a soft kiss on the palm.

We fall back into a peaceful silence as the movie plays on, his hand still interlocking with mine while his thumb absent-mindedly draws circles on the back of my hand. I can't stop staring at him, and honestly, I'm not really sure that I want to. I always make fun of the characters in my smutty romance novels for falling for the main guy so easily. Yet, here I am on a first date, and I'm already absolutely head over heels for this man.

The movie comes to an end, and I catch myself wanting to whine and complain that it's over. Cameron smiles blithely and looks at me with contentment. I get out of the car and fold up the blanket and hand it to Cam who walks around his car to grab it from me.

"I got it, thanks," Cam says softly with a smile that doesn't quite reach his eyes. He opens the door for me again before walking around to the back of his car, placing the items in the trunk, closing it, then returning to the driver's seat. I get this weird feeling in the pit of my stomach, shaking my head, realizing that I'm just being dramatic.

I jump slightly, not expecting his door to close while lost in my own thoughts. We drive back to my place in each other's quiet company. I'm not upset about it either. Tonight has been *perfect*. Tonight was something I never thought my broken soul could ever have.

A tension begins to permeate the car.

I glance over at Cameron, his shoulders seem tighter than before, his brow furrows. I want to ask what's wrong. I want to take his hand again and hold it like we did at the movies. His face looks like he's battling some inner-demon, and I don't even know what I can do to help him, or fix this.

11
FALLING

LEYLA

Pulling up to my house and parking in front, there's a charged air in the car that I can't quite place nor do I know what caused it. I feel almost dizzy from the whiplash it gives me; going from tense to charged in what seems to be the blink of an eye. There's definitely something going on with him that he's not saying. I try to turn away so it doesn't seem like I'm staring at him again, but our eyes catch, his eyes darken, and a smirk grows on his face.

"See something you like?" Cam teases me. I bite my lower lip and chuckle. Cam runs his hands through his hair, then squeezes the back of his neck still fighting some internal battle that he's trying to push aside. The tone of his voice isn't the same lighthearted one it was just an hour ago.

I make the executive decision to change the entire outcome right now by letting him know that I really do want him with me right now. Feeding his ego just a bit, hoping that it'll convince him to come inside with me.

"Just this pretty nice guy, kinda tall, dorky smile..." I tease him right back, though my voice betrays the nerves that I am definitely still feeling. The date was perfect, and I smile back at him but I still can't shake this nagging feeling. He's honestly too good to be true. Should that be some sort of warning?

"Oh yea? Tell me more, Cherry, because what you think I do to you..." there's a pause as his gaze rakes over me, "doesn't even begin to reach the surface of how much you do to me." His voice is practically shaking with forced restraint as his face moves closer to mine.

"I'm pretty sure I do, but why don't you tell me anywa-" My words are cut off by the swiftness of his lips crashing into mine. It's hard, fast, and not at all the gentleness that his eyes had shown earlier, but it's fierce, powerful, and tortured.

"*Fuck*, Cherry," he groans as he kisses me harder, moving his kisses down my chin to the side of my neck. My breath quickens as he does, I tilt my head giving him access and his tongue circles my pulse point and he gently bites. A breathy moan escapes my lips, my own hand gently rakes along his thigh. The air in the car changes, it's charged but not like before. It's hot and full of need.

His breath hitching as I lean into his kisses, pressing on his jeans. His cock already straining against his jeans, begging for release.

"Leyla—" his voice is breathy, a rasp to it that betrays all pretense of the respectful man he was earlier.

I want a redo. I *need* a redo— to make up for the nightmare that was the other day; but most of all, I need a release.

I pull away, backing myself into my seat once again and I turn to him. I bite my lower lip, seeing the passion flaring in his eyes.

"Cameron–please—" My hands fidget with his pants, as his head falls away from me, his tortured eyes burning into my soul. He nods and I take a breath. "*Here*, or there." I jut my thumb toward the front door of my apartment building, and he grins, knowing that the second option is definitely the better of the two.

"You've already consumed every waking thought and I need to make this a fucking reality." He takes a deep breath, failing to compose himself.

"Yours. *Now*."

He fumbles to unlock his door, and quickly makes his way to my side opening the door for me, then we're off.

I'm giggling like a mad woman as he leads me into the lobby of my apartment, we run up the flight of stairs, stealing desperate kisses as we go. I'm prepared this time, I unlock my door and take the lead and pull him into my room, I don't want him to think that there's any other outcome for right now.

"*Cherry*," Cameron pants as he stares at me, my grin widens. "I need to know what you want right now Ley, cause the things I want to do to you aren't kind, sweet or gentle." I let out a soft gasp as I hear his words, sending a shiver down my spine. But that clearly won't do.

I lock eyes with him and smirk. "I promise you, I don't need that. I don't *want* that. Right now? I just want you."

Cameron groans as he looks at me, his pupils wide and the green of them basically consumed by the wanton desire that is present on his face. He lets out a growl that is almost inhuman. I yelp as he lunges towards me, pushing me onto my bed.

"Cameron—Cam—" I moan, his body hovers over me and he's on me in a second. His mouth latches to my neck and my nails dig into his muscular back as his tongue bathes over me, sucking and nipping away. *"Ohh,"* I pant but push him back.

"Cam, let me do this for you." In no way am I strong, but I flip us over so that Cameron is on his back and I'm now kneeling over him.

"Leyla..." he protests, but that doesn't stop me from running my hands up and down his chest. He looks at me with a pained look, his cock throbbing, demanding release from its denim prison. I am more than happy to oblige, my eyes connecting with his. I know what needs to be done, I lean across and begin trailing kisses down his jaw to his neck as he tries to prop himself up again.

"No Cam, please let me do this for you. This— just let me." Cam lies there panting, but reluctantly nods, as I lean down and unzip his jeans. He lets out a breath as he lifts up his hips as I pull down his pants, his boxers the next thing to be torn from his perfect body. I adjust myself over him, and my eyes widen slightly as his cock pulses erect against his abs. I take in the fucking gorgeous man in front of me.

"Let me take care of you," I say again, more breathlessly as I bend over him, taking his cock in one hand, as my tongue licks the pre-cum beading on the head.

His hips buck, as I swirl my tongue over his head. "Be a good boy and stay still for me."

———

Cameron

I'm going to fucking die. This woman is going to be the death of me, she will be my undoing. If she does that thing with her tongue again, I am going to come apart before I have the chance to even start.

She's kneeling over me and then her hands are on my hips and her tongue is lathing over my cock. My hands fist her comforter as she plunges her mouth onto my cock. My cock twitches from the unexpected contact, she lets out a throaty giggle, that sends vibrations through me, threatening to explode like a fucking teenager getting his first blow job.

"L-Leyla," I stammer out knowing damn well that I am a goner if she keeps this up. My hips buck up, she gags as she takes me even deeper, her eyes clearly fighting back tears as she struggles to take my entire length in her mouth.

"Leyla— *stop*," I force out. She immediately pulls herself off of my cock, and the absence of her mouth on me leaves me aching. I need to be inside her, I need to show her that she's mine. My cock rests on my stomach, as I sit up I know that if I didn't stop now this would all be for naught. "On your back, Cherry. Let me show you what you do to me."

She nods as she crawls over me, still kissing me up my chest as she then lays herself down next to me on her king bed, her eyes full of sex and I am going to make sure she knows exactly what she's going to get with me. I pull her pants off and slip on the condom I grabbed from my wallet a moment ago.

"I don't do safe words, you want to stop, you tell me to stop, okay?" She nods, and whimpers as she reaches for me. I make my way to her pussy and a dark smile forms on my face.

"Cherry, you're fucking drenched. Is this all for me?"

She whimpers again, nodding while biting one of her fingers. Her other hand reaches for her tits as she taunts me, teasing her nipple. I don't give her a moment to think or realize what I'm doing as I crawl over her and shove my cock inside her soaked pussy.

"*Cam!*" Leyla screams out as I thrust into her at a bruising pace. Her back arches and her hands fly around me, nails scraping down my back.

"You take my cock so well, baby. You were made for me." I can feel her squeezing my cock as she moves her hips in time with mine, I lean down and take her nipple in my mouth and bite down on it as she bucks her hips in both pain and pleasure.

"I'm— I'm— I'm gonna—" Leyla moans as I feel her pussy clenching around my cock. My balls constrict, begging me to unload and claim what is *mine.*

"Come for me, Cherry— come with me." I groan against the shell of her ear, my thrusts unrelenting as she screams. The force of her orgasm wraps around my cock like a vice and my own release finds me as we fall into oblivion together. I pull myself out of her when I know that she's finished, satisfaction finding me at the sight of her abused, dripping, cunt. Her breath is unsteady, her arm covers her face as she tries to control her breathing. Leyla's body is limp, her breaths still staggered and uneven, but I smile as I kiss the inside of her thigh.

"You are fucking perfect, Cherry. Fucking stunning." I ease myself off her bed as she looks like she's finally coming to. I can't help this stupid grin that grows on my face knowing that it was me that forced her to ruin. I sneak into her attached bathroom and get a towel, walk back over to her, and find her sitting on the edge of her bed. The effects of what we'd just done dripping down her legs.

"Cameron, I think that was…" she lets out a breath, her face still flushed red, as she looks me over. "Woah." The docile look on her face gives me a sort of rush that has me nearly ready to go again.

We get cleaned up and we both are floating after what I can only explain as the come down from the best orgasm of my life. A dopey grin still on my face as we make our way out of the bedroom. Leyla follows behind me like a lovesick puppy. The things I currently am feeling don't match what is swimming around in my brain, but I don't care. She sits at the island in her kitchen, her body languid and relaxed as I get her a glass of water.

"You okay, Cherry-girl?" I place the glass in front of her, smile, and sit on the stool next to her, my hand gently touching her cheek while she smiles back at me.

"Yea, I'm great. Like this was definitely the best date I've ever been on." Leyla smiles sleepily at me, as she takes a sip of her water. "We should definitely do this again." I feel everything fall into place, everything was finally the way it should've been so long ago. Except now there's one thing that's right where it should be.

She's finally *mine*.

12

TEA, ROSES, AND PASTS

LEYLA

Cameron and I spend the next couple weeks with each other. Most of our time is spent at my apartment but I like waking up at his place too. Something about being wrapped up in his sheets with his arms around me, the smell of him encompassing me, it makes me feel a little more whole than I've been in a long time. I find myself smiling more and even my therapist has noticed a positive change in me.

Cam brings me little gifts, whether it's my favorite candy, or a new book from the bookstore. It's the little things that add up that make me feel like I'm the luckiest girl in the world. My mind wanders as I'm sitting at the cafe working on my assignments for the week. I'm trying to get ahead of the workload because Cam said he's got a little trip planned for us this weekend. I can't wait.

I laugh to myself quietly thinking about the message that Cameron sent me earlier today and roll my eyes because of what a lovesick fool this man is. I click back to my assignment when I feel my phone vibrate. It's Detective Alexandra. I take a deep breath and answer it.

"Hey, Detective," I say, a soft smile on my face, my heart racing slightly when I talk to her because I never know if it's a good or bad call. "Everything okay?"

A deeper laugh on the other end loosens my nerves, "How many times have I told you to call me Alex?"

I let out a laugh and shrug, knowing full well she can't see me. "I know, I know. I feel like I can't do that with you, it's out of respect!" I run my hand through my hair and laugh softly. "What's going on Alex? Any news? What's going on with the Program? Is it about my parent's case?" The questions spew out of me like actual vomit, uncontrollable and messy. She sighs softly.

The line sits quiet for a moment and that charged feeling settles into me again, but it's quickly broken by Detective Alexandra's voice. "We haven't had any updates on your folks' case, but I did want you to know they do think The Whispering Killer is possibly active again. We don't have anything concrete on it, but the M.O. is the same. And while you know I can't tell you everything, as it's an ongoing investigation, just stay alert. Okay, dear? I worry about you being back in town alone."

A small smile creeps onto my face when I know it shouldn't be. Calm settles over me knowing that maybe working so closely with Alex lets me realize that, I probably shouldn't be worrying so much, I'm working so closely with one of the best women in law enforcement.

"Well about *that*," I say, bringing focus to her closing statement. Talking about boys is definitely favorable to talking about a killer. *The* killer. At least it'll put her mind at ease, and I desperately want to hold onto the high Cameron's had me on. "I'm actually, well, I'm kinda seeing someone. You had a bit of a... play in our relationship."

The silence on the other end of the phone makes me nervous, my fingers start playing with the hem of my shirt, rubbing it is a bit of comfort. But when Alexandra speaks, you can hear the smile in her voice. She giggles, too. "I always knew you two would end up together!"

We talk on the phone for another twenty minutes. I tell her all about Cameron, how even though it's only been three weeks, he pays attention and is attentive to all my needs. He buys me little things that remind him of me and things that he thinks I would like. "He's really fantastic! Cameron really is such a good guy, and I'm really glad to have reconnected with him. He really makes Maplewood feel like home again, makes me feel safe." I sigh dreamily just thinking about him when the air changes again around me.

"I'm so happy for you, gorgeous girl. I'm glad things are going well for you. Maybe moving home from Chicago was just what you needed." There's an intonation in her voice that I really should pay more attention to, but I ignore it as I try to keep my focus on the conversation. Now more than ever, though, I feel the need to end this call.

I look around anxiously but there's no one in the cafe so I shake it off and go to end the call as nonchalantly as I can. Something feels wrong, and it's a feeling that since coming home has been happening more often and I can't help but feel like something bad is happening around me.

"Yea, it really was. Well, I've gotta get back to my school-work, but maybe if you're free at all we can meet up for dinner? We can talk soon?" I blunder out, hoping it doesn't sound too forced.

"Of course, beautiful girl. I'd love to catch up soon— not program related. You tell that boy he best be treating you right, or he's got to face the wrath of me." Alexandra chuckles, but I smile anyway, knowing that though she's trying to come off as she's joking, she's also not in the same sentence. "Stay healthy, love. We'll talk soon." We finally hang up, and I let out a breath that feels as if I've not been taking full inhales all day.

I look at the time, it's only 2:30 P.M. I'm not meeting up with Cameron until 7 P.M., so I focus back on my assignments as best I can. I put my headphones back on my head and blast some Noah Kahan, to help calm my nerves, which are definitely still on high alert. But, also, I can't help but feel better when listening to him.

———

A few hours pass and I'm working, minding my own business, when a shadow covers me. A chill rolls through my body— there's someone sitting at the table with me. A taller man, he's around my age, black hair, and pitch-colored eyes, like they're soulless. He smiles at me. There's something unsettling about the smile, but I return a nervous smile trying to be polite.

"Well, I'll be damned. I had heard that you came home, but

I had to see it with my own eyes." The man adjusts his black rimmed glasses, which look like they're a size too big for his face. I tilt my head at him in confusion, moving my headphones to rest around my neck.

"I have come home, yeah, but I can't say that I know who you are... Am I supposed to?" The tone of my voice is distant and cold; I don't exactly make a habit of being cozy with complete strangers. But I guess he's not, according to him. I look at him, really look at him, hoping these random puzzle pieces will fit into place as to who the fuck this man is.

"Well, haha, I would hope you'd remember me! It's Simon– Simon Maher– we used to go to group together. We were friends!" He looks at me as if those words are supposed to make everything fall into place when I'm only more and more confused. In group, I never really had many friends except for Hazel, and later on in time, Cameron. I haven't the slightest idea who he is.

My smile is more of a grimace, I feel slightly bad when I look back at Simon. "I'm so sorry, I can't say that I remember you. But I'm sure we did know each other! You stuck around Maplewood?" I force out, trying to be polite, but I get an uncomfortable feeling wafting off of him.

"Aww, you should know who I am! Honestly, I'm hurt you don't remember me. I'm actually back in town to help out with this new Group Outreach Program. Detective Alexandra asked me to help out."

I can't quite tell if he is feigning fake hurt to be lighthearted, or if he is actually upset about it. I watch as Simon pulls out his phone and pulls up a group photo of the kids from the group I had gone to. Front and center is Cameron. Standing next to him was a kid with dirty blonde hair. Simon points to him, "That's me! I've just... grown up a bit."

How the supposed to bring up the fact he was somehow expecting me to remember someone who I had met in passing so many years ago?

This is quite likely the most awkward conversation of my life, but looking over the photo, little snippets of my childhood come flashing back to me. I begin to slowly remember bits and pieces of him; he was friends with Cameron, and... maybe the guy's name was Spencer? No– Ryann. I do remember him, I look up at Simon and a softer smile sits on my face now.

"Oh my gosh, I do remember you! What a small world, I'm helping with Detective Alex's program too. And so is Cameron. Oh you know, I'm actually hanging out with Cameron later today!" I say with a little pep in my voice, a genuine smile forming on my face as I look at Simon, who's body tenses up. "We should all plan a day to hang out and catch up soon." Literally thinking of Cameron makes these ridiculous butterflies come up at the worst moments. I shake my head, and look back up at Simon who hasn't moved or said a word.

He looks at me and puts on a smile again. "Yea, that'd be nice. I should go." Without another word, Simon gets up from the table and walks out of the cafe. I sit there staring at the door for a moment trying to figure out what the fuck just happened. The whole interaction had been... *bizarre.*

I take a deep breath and immediately start packing up my things to leave. I still don't quite know what just happened, but

I want to go home and wholly do not want to be around people anymore.

Tonight's quiet date with Cameron cannot come soon enough.

> Leyla: God, what a weird fucking day. I cannot WAIT to see you tonight. You'll never guess who I just ran into!!!!!!!

The message goes unread for a while, which is a little unlike Cameron, but I'm sure it's nothing. He's probably just working and can't get to his phone. The interaction with Simon has my mind running a mile a minute and I honestly feel like I'm just a little more on edge than normal. Maybe this is just how it is when I think a little too hard on childhood, like Simon just forced me to do. So much for all the work I've been doing in therapy.

I walk out of the cafe to start heading home. It's only a few blocks away but the chilly October air has definitely started to set in, and I make a mental note that I should pull out my heavier sweaters. I quicken my pace and hurry home, both to start getting ready for our date, and to get out of the cold. I finally get home and when I make it upstairs, I have this horrible feeling in the pit of my stomach.

A cold gust of air hits me as I walk through the front door of my apartment, and sitting smack in the middle of the floor of my place is a fucking funeral bouquet. A photo of my parents positioned in the middle of it. I can't fucking breathe. I feel the walls closing in on me.

It's October 21st. The day my parents were murdered. The

day that changed my whole life, and I had been so wrapped up in my own head that I didn't fucking realize that it was today.

My parents' death anniversary is today. The person who's been stalking me since I was sixteen did this weird flower shit again, and this time it wasn't just left somewhere outside, or in public without me seeing. They had been *in* my home. I stave off the impending panic attack and try to call someone, anyone. My fingers fumble my phone out and I press the first number that pops up. He answers on the first ring.

"Hey you–" Cam cuts himself off and the only sound on the line is me, hyperventilating. "Leyla?"

I can't speak, the world around me is spinning, and my chest feels ungodly tight. I think I can hear Cam talking on the phone, but I'm not sure. I sit on the floor of my apartment, fully unaware of how much time has passed. I flinch as the door to my apartment flies open.

"Hey– Hey, Cherry..." Cameron's soft voice pulls me out of my disassociation. Had he been close by or something? Was it time for our date? I'm so out of it, I don't really know what's happening, but he's here. He's here with me, he's here.

"Baby, what's wrong– what ha– *what the fuck?*" I watch his eyes fall on the floral arrangement lying on the floor behind me. His face pales as he looks at me. "Leyla, I need you to tell me what happened, okay?"

He hedges then. "Let me take care of this, you don't even have to worry about it."

Cameron's jaw ticks as he looks at the arrangement, he immediately scoops me up in his arms, and carries me to my bed, where he crouches down in front of me. "Cherry, you stay

here, okay?I'm gonna get rid of that, and then I'll be right back."
I absentmindedly nod, my eyes following him as he picks up the
flowers then disappears out the door.

I close my eyes for just a moment, and the next time they
open, it's the next day. I'm awoken by the soft breath of another
on my cheek. Someone's arms are wrapped tightly around me
and I feel safe. I slowly turn over so that I'm facing Cam. He
stayed, the entire night he stayed, and didn't leave me alone. I
cuddle into his warmth reflexively, laying in contentment. Cam
must have felt me stir, as his arms squeeze me, then he's slowly
pushing off me and glancing down at me.

"Hey, Cherry, you okay?" His brows bunch, a little crease
forms on his forehead.

"Yea, yea, I'm okay... I-I didn't mean to bother you... I'm so
sorry... You should go Cameron— I mean it's okay if you *want* to
go. I'd absolutely understand if you didn't want to be here..."
I'm primed to keep going but he slaps his hand over my mouth
gingerly and laughs just as softly.

"Leyla, let me make one thing very clear. I want you— your
fears, your anxieties, your happiness— *you*. There is nowhere
else in this world that I'd rather be than right here." Cameron
reaches out and runs his hand through my hair. His touch alone
is all the comfort I need at this moment. But I don't deserve it.

"Uh, *no*. This is the second fucking time you've had to come
to my rescue. Clearly, my life is a mess, I'm an even bigger mess,
and there are so many other people out there who would be *so*
much more mentally stable than I am." My voice gets stronger
as I go on, my insecurities pushing their way through to the
forefront of my emotions.

Cameron sits me up, grabs my chin, making me look him in the eyes. "You don't have to exist in your pain alone, okay? I'm here because I want to be here. I want to be around you, spend time with you, and learn all about *you*. You are magnificent. You're so fucking smart, funny and brave... Being with you is the most alive I've felt in years."

He removes his hand from my chin and gently rubs the back of his finger across my cheek. "You can run, scream, and push me away all you want, Cherry; but I promise you that I will stop at nothing to prove you are *mine*."

I exhale and blink, leaning in slowly, and placing a soft kiss on his lips.

"I'm yours," I whisper, brushing his lips with my own. He adjusts his legs on the bed so that there's space for me. He holds his arms open and without hesitation I'm in them. Being surrounded by his warmth and safety is something that I can get used to. I *want* to get used to it.

I sit in his arms for what feels like forever, and once my heart isn't going to explode out of my chest, I look at him and smile softly. My hands gently tracing over his arms. He must feel me staring, because his emerald eyes connect with mine as my smile widens and he smiles too.

"Hey," I whisper out, the smile still not leaving my face.

"Hey, Cherry," Cameron whispers back to me, gently placing a kiss on my forehead. "So, what'd you do yesterday?" He says sweetly, not once breaking eye contact with me. His smile and that damn dimple appears, and I instantly feel the calm settle over me. I melt into him and look up.

"I got some homework done, spent it at the cafe yesterday."

I purse my lips, scrunching my face as I think about what else I did yesterday besides come home to my literal nightmare. "*Oh!* You'll never guess who I ran into at the cafe. Simon Maher, from group. Literally don't know what's in the water, but he's definitely just as weird as he was when we were kids." I scoff and shrug. "But I'm being too judgy, aren't I? Maybe we should plan a day to hang out soon. I could use some friends in town."

"No shit? Yea, we would hang out all the time when we were kids. I'm kinda shocked he's back in town, I haven't seen him in years." Cam looks down at me and smiles, "We can definitely see if Simon wants to meet up for drinks or something. Plus, I've got a little surprise planned for you, so this could be fun to include him in my secret plans for you," he teases me and gently places a kiss on my cheek.

"What secret plans do you have in store for me?" I query and pull out of his hold, but Cameron's having none of it and ropes me back into his embrace. I laugh playfully, but he just gives me a gentle squeeze.

"That's for me to know and you to find out," Cameron teases once more, and I let out a laugh. "But for tonight, it's just us now, okay? I'm not leaving you alone. I mean, if you're okay with—"

"Yes—absolutely yes… please stay," my voice is trying to hide the underlying panic from seeping in too much. "Stay, Cam."

So he does.

CLOSE CALL

THE WHISPERING KILLER

That was too fucking close of a call. Too fucking close. She's getting suspicious, but I must do everything I can to keep her off my trail. I was working in the shop today.

I walk back into my space and see the man unconscious and tied up. I can't help the grin that grows on my face seeing the palette of colors blooming on his skin from our earlier sessions. I take my jobs seriously. I know who, *what* I am, and I know exactly what's expected of me to make *her* proud.

"Liam Masterson! Wakey, wakey!" I shout into his ear, startling the gagged man awake. "Our time was interrupted, and we can't let that happen now can we!" I let out a laugh that I see sends chills up the whimpering fool's body.

He begins to thrash around as I turn my back to him, walking my fingers over my tools that lie on the table next to him. The air is sterile, cold, and unfeeling, as I grab a small knife and gently twist it around. Turning to stare at the man, intimidating him as I twist the knife again between my fingers, play checking the sharpness of the tool.

"Tell me, Liam. Did your victims beg for mercy?" I take the knife and gently drag it down his arm, blood slowly pooling up along the slice. "Did you even listen to them? Tell me, Liam, what went through your head when you were killing those girls? Did it make you feel stronger? More like a *man*?" I turn around clenching my fist, thinking about all that was done to *her* and the anger begins to flood into me.

A vein ticks in my jaw as I take a deep breath and look back at Liam, his body fighting against the restraints. A bit of pride runs through me knowing that he isn't going anywhere.

"What do you think, Liam, are you gonna hurt another girl? Or can we surmise that you learned your lesson?" The knife trails along his cheek, as a grin once again forms on my face. The knife slices through the gag I had in place, allowing Liam to speak.

The man's eyes widen as he immediately begins to grovel, "P-Please! *Please!* I promise you— I swear! I'll never do it again! I've learned m-m-my lesson! I'm done for good!" Liam stammers out, as the pathetic man screams for his life.

"See, that wasn't so hard! I'll happily let you go," I say with glee as I turn to him. I then take the knife and stab him in the jugular, a satisfying *splurt* sounding out for only my ears. The man's body goes limp moments later while his blood garbles. His life-force slips away with every drop of crimson and the world is now free from yet another man who caused more pain.

I grab the man's chin, forcing his unseeing eyes, burning

into my soul, the color fading from his body. I whisper, "I will stop at nothing, to rid the world of useless trash like you. Never again." I open my supply cabinet and immediately begin to dispose of his body. This is honestly my favorite part of it all. The after— the control of knowing exactly what has to happen. Knowing exactly what to do and how to dispose of all of it and never get caught.

Clean. In all sense of the word. I fold up the plastic tarp and place it so that the blood won't leave its confines. The body is cleaned up and ready for disposal in no time flat; though the speed is from practice and precision, not rush and panic.

When my hands are clean and my mind is completely quiet, I pull out my journal and write down the details of everything that was done today, and a sense of pride fills me that I can't help but wonder if they'd be proud of me. A warmth fills me as I know in my heart that *she* most certainly would be.

I have to see her again.

14
CHAI & PANCAKES
CAMERON

Spending time with Leyla has honestly become my favorite pastime. I'm so fucking lucky that she's back in my life, she's incredible. I hate the fact that she's going through so much, and she thinks she has to go through it alone.

We lay in bed, and the soft tickle of her breath hits my neck as I pull her close to me. Instinctively, she nuzzles in closer.

Perfection. This woman is fucking perfect. The cherry on top being that she's fucking mine. I could lay here forever knowing that she's the one in my arms. I'm the one holding her. Mine, mine, mine. *Mine.*

Leyla begins to stir and her beautiful eyes, all content and sleepy, gaze up at me. I run a hand through her hair and smile back at her. "Sleep well, baby?" My dimple makes an appearance, her face instantly heating when she sees it. I love the way my girl responds to the simplest things.

Leyla nods sleepily, pulling herself closer to me and kissing my bare chest. "Yea, I think it's safe to say that's probably the best I've slept in... well, in a while."

My heart hurts for her knowing that she's losing sleep over something that never had anything to do with her, but left her alone and feeling broken. My mouth turns into a frown, as she looks up at me with wonder in her beautifully mismatched eyes. "Why didn't you tell me that you haven't been sleeping?"

She shrugs, and I can actually see her walls slowly forming back up. I grab her by the chin, not wanting her to shut me out. "How about this Cherry: go take a shower. And while you're in there, I'll make us some breakfast. How do... pancakes sound?"

Her body softens against me and the light slowly returns to her eyes. I let out a sigh of relief as she nods to me, gently pulling away, and immediately I'm missing the warmth of her body connecting with mine. She looks at me with that smile that could send me to my knees. "You're beautiful, Cherry."

The red creeps up her neck again, and blood instantly goes right to my cock. I wish she knew the things she does to me— without intention; with simply being herself. Leyla whispers something softly and turns around and heads off to the bathroom. Once I hear the shower start, I plop back into the pillows letting out a groan. Then force myself up, my erection not at all hidden, padding over towards the kitchen and begin cooking our breakfast.

I am so fucking into this woman, and she doesn't even know the extent of it. I wonder if it would terrify her.

―――――――

I have no fucking idea where Cameron Curtis came from, but he is so fucking perfect that I can't even begin to describe it. I think I've fallen for this man. Is that even possible when we've only been together for a couple of weeks now? I look at the mirror after my shower, the condensation from the steam still blurring my view. I use the edge of the towel to clear away a little section so I can see my reflection in the mirror. I brush my hair and pull out two hair ties, and begin braiding my hair down the back.

———

By the time I walk out of the bathroom, I can smell the food that Cameron's made for us. *Not only is he beautiful inside and out, but he can cook too?!*

I can't help but walk out with a beaming smile on my face, as I make my way to the two island stools where he's setting out the plates for us. The way he looks at me is something you see in the movies. The light in his eyes illuminates every detail of his face— *because of me.* It makes my stomach do somersaults and my heart beats against the walls of my chest in a near nauseating rhythm.

Part of me feels like I don't deserve him. It's as if he can almost sense the insecurities and his arms are around me in a second, and he's kissing my neck.

"Hope you're hungry, baby girl," He purrs into my ear and a shiver racks my spine. I let out a soft, affirming grunt as he leads me to the stool and sits me down.

"Whatever you made smells delicious." My eyes rove over

the counter in front of me and widen when he runs over to the stove and pours something into a mug for me.

"Chai, just how you like it." Cameron smiles as he places it in front of me and my chest tightens with some unknown feeling. I beam up at him and can't help it when he looks at me expectantly. I grab the orange mug and take a sip, letting the warm and spicy liquid ignite every tastebud I have with its *perfect* balance and sweetness.

"Holy fuck Cam," I say incredulously as he looks at me with a smile that matches my own. "This is the best chai I've ever had."

He cooks, knows how to properly make chai, knows how to manage a panic attack, and he's a fucking gentleman. I send my thanks to whatever is watching out for me from up above, because I've hit the damn jackpot with this man.

We sit and talk about life— school mostly— while eating our breakfast and I cannot take my eyes off of him. We finally hit a lull in the conversation, which is fine with me because I've just about eaten so much that I could die.

"You ready for today, Cherry? Because your surprise should be here... In..." he looks down checking his phone with a smirk, "about thirty seconds."

My eyes widen from confusion before glaring at him analytically. "Cameron Curtis— what have you done?"

Before he even has a chance to answer, I hear nothing other than my best friend banging on the door yelling, "*Open the door, Leyley!* We got shit to do!"

My heart does that thing where it feels like it's going to explode out of my chest and I don't even know where to go from here. The banging from Hazel continues with her attempts getting more persistent. I let out a choked laugh.

"Better let her in before she breaks down the damn door," Cameron says with crinkled eyes and a five-star smile.

If I wasn't already sure that I was in love with this man before, I sure as shit was absolutely positive now. I'm so overcome with affection and excitement, I feel like I could lick his face. But, I settle for a quick kiss on his lips, then I run to the door, fling it open, and am immediately bombarded by my tiny terror of a best friend.

This is perfect.

15

JUST WHAT I NEED

LEYLA

"**B**ITCH! When did you get so hot?! Like you were hot before, but you are *hotttttt,*" Hazel drags out the last word as she looks me over. Then her eyes connect with Cameron and a cat-like grin overtakes her tawny face. "Well, well, well. The infamous Cameron Curtis."

Hazel lets go of me and the size difference between the two of them is almost comical. Hazel is maybe five-foot-three on a good day, and Cameron's clearing six-foot-two easy. The way Hazel is probably more intimidating, though, makes me laugh.

"It's good to see you again, Hazel." Cameron nods his head politely towards Hazel's assessing stare. To Cameron's credit, he doesn't balk or move away; and even more to his credit, he smiles wide. "I haven't filled her in on any of the plans. I thought I would give you the honor."

The fact that my best friend and boyfriend are already scheming behind my back has me feeling some sort of way.

Genuine surprise, like the feel it in your bones and down to your toes kind of surprised. I can't remember the last time that I felt this way *and* it wasn't under the lens of what had happened to me when I was a kid, instead coming from the fact that it's by two people who care about me. It's something that I can definitely get used to. Hazel's eyes grow ten sizes as she looks at me with her scheming face— a look that I had grown to know all too well during our teen years.

"Hazel, Cam... What are you two planning...?" I try to hide a smile as I look between the two.

Cam's got this shit-eating grin on his face that makes me almost nervous, but I know that it's so going to be worth it. Hazel pulls me onto my couch; with an *oomph*, we plop down and Hazel beams up at me, pulling me into yet another bone crushing hug. Cameron follows us, perched on the arm and watching us with a smile as warm as the afternoon sun. *Wow, I've got it bad. Stay focused, Ley.*

"One, I missed you so much! You look fucking stunning! And two, we're going to a rage room!" Hazel says with so much excitement, as my face looks at her slightly confused, but I plaster on a smile.

"A... rage room? What's that, like a room with a therapist that forces you to get angry or something weird like that?" I look at her not understanding what she's even talking about.

Cameron lets out a soft chuckle from next to me, but Hazel shoots him a momentary glare before looking back to me. "A rage room is like–this room where you go to break shit. You've been dealing with literally so much lately. Cam and I figured that this would be something fun for you to get your pent-up emotions out. Let's break some shit!"

My, no doubt, incredulous face sends Hazel into a frenzy of laughter. I force myself to keep a straight face knowing full well that this is a losing game for the both of us. I look at her deadpan and she sighs with exasperation.

"Leyley, you know I love you. But you need to *let loose!* What better way than breaking a bunch of shit?" Hazel looks at me with a murderous gleam in her eye.

"Fine. *Fine.*" I relent as Hazel squeals with excitement, and Cameron lets out a quiet laugh. I look back at Cameron smiling, his laugh melting through me and soothing me like a balm to my soul.

I don't know what it is about seeing two people I care about being together, but I feel *complete.* Like all the pieces I've been slowly falling into, they are here to put me back together. With care and gentleness that I'm just getting accustomed to thanks to Cameron. All the heaviness in my life that has suddenly reared its ugly head as of late, so it's nice to have things be quiet for a moment. It's nice to feel like this place could be home for me.

Then again, it's more about the people than the location, isn't it?

16

CHOKEHOLD

LEYLA

The three of us head towards Cameron's car. He didn't bring the Maserati today which slightly bums me out; though, he mentioned that it was getting detailed. Cameron opened the door for Hazel, her smile beaming, although her eyes portrayed skepticism. Making his way over to me, Cameron smiles and *lovingly* places a kiss on my lips. I can't describe how I know it's lovingly other than I just *feel* it.

"You okay, Cherry?" he whispers, eyeing my carefully. Over his shoulder, I can see Hazel glaring at him with dramatic incredulity.

Failing at totally holding back my laugh, I am chuckling a bit as I reply, "Yea babe, I'm fine. Overwhelmed, but a good overwhelmed." Cameron watches me with his grin growing to goofy proportions.

Even though I want to get lost in today with them and fully

let go just like they want me to, I can't deny a heaviness that's still on my chest. And before I get in the car and start this day with the two of them, I need to be honest with Cameron about it. I fidget with the fabric of his shirt as I pull him nearer, all the while avoiding eye contact. "I think I'm still exhausted from last night. I can't shake the feeling that someone's watching me. Like no matter where I turn someone... is watching me."

A shiver runs through my body as Cameron's hands run up and down my arms. A gentle caress is a feeling that I don't know how to process. He's almost too good to be true.

"Cherry, I know what happened yesterday was horrible. I know your sanctuary was tainted by darkness, and they took away your feeling of safety. I hate that there was no way for me to prevent this..." He bites his lip and it seems like he drifts off for a moment. When he comes back, he's focused and intense in the eyes, while his hands remain gentle. "After our fun today, why don't we sit down and order you some security equipment for your apartment? A doorbell camera, window alarms, and any other neat gadget the internet comes up with. That way, none of this can happen again." Cameron's voice is so soft and careful, yet strong and affirming at the same time.

I try to fight the burning in my eyes from what this man is doing for me— to me. "Yea— yea, I think that will be good." Clearing my throat from the tightness that was creeping into it, I continue. "I think maybe it's time to tell Alex, too– Detective Alexandra, I mean. But that's something I can do later."

It's almost imperceivable but something flashes over Cameron's face though it's gone in a moment. Cam's eyes connect with mine, as he starts moving his hands down my arms once again. "Okay, now take a deep breath and shake out your hands."

He gently grabs onto my clenched hands and opens them up, interlacing our fingers. I nod and listen intently to his words, a deep breath in and out, then a shake of my arms. Once I'm done, he pulls my hands up to his lips and kisses each knuckle. A moment of silence passes between the two of us, my shoulders curve inwards with relief.

"Such a good girl." Cam beams at me, my worries and fears slipping away. "Let's go before Hazel starts complaining." He opens up the front car door for me, letting me get in. I turn around to a stunned Hazel who sat in the backseat of the car with the world's most devious smile.

"Girl, you got it *bad,*" Hazel blurts out before Cameron gets into the driver's seat. Heat creeps up my cheeks as I turn back around wishing there was a way for me to crawl into a hole. Cameron turns to me with a knowing grin, and I laugh awkwardly.

"Okay, we ready?" Cam queries as he backs out of the parking spot. When there are no objections, we head off to the rage room just forty-five minutes out of town. The ride there is anything but quiet, as Cameron puts on some playlist with songs from the 2000's. Hazel's and my eyes light up, Cameron's lips twitch into a dorky smile that ignites my blood like a powder keg. *I could just eat him up.*

We sing our hearts out, Cameron joining in on a couple songs and I'm almost sad that our ride is coming to an end. The three of us make our way to the rental desk; unabashedly, I'm all smile as we walk in.

The three of us walk into the rage room and we're immediately bombarded with the sounds of alternative music echoing through the space. From *Ashes to Embers* is setting the tone for the day and making this all feel like fate— I've been *obsessed* with this band for months. It has me grinning like a mad woman. Cameron breaks off from our little trio to finish something with the man who checked us in.

Hazel whirls to face me, her eyes burning a hole into my soul. I flinch preemptively to the impending outburst. "One, what the fuck?! You've been holding out on me how *good* this man is! Like, since when did he become such a gentleman instead of some dorky kid that skulked around group?!" Hazel whisper yells at me as she hits me playfully. "Two, you're *actually* falling for him, aren't you? 'Cause after what I just saw when we left, fuck I think I might be falling for him if you aren't." Her final words are swoony and breathy as she tosses a glance in Cameron's direction.

My face fully doesn't portray the thousand emotions raging war with one another inside of my chest—*a hot spike of jealousy being new.* I know she's joking and trying to get a rise out of me, and I hate how easy it is. Should it be a red flag I'm feeling this strongly already? *Stop.* I'm trying to ruin my own day. A day that the woman in front of me, and the man who is stealing my heart at record speed, planned for me.

A smile curves from my pursed lips, letting out a soft laugh. "I am, Haze– like, it's so bad, he's been fucking nothing but a gentleman. He's made me breakfast, fucked me senseless, and also gave me the best cuddles after a panic attack."

I look at her exasperated, throwing my hands up, putting on

a fake temper tantrum with no real malice in my actions. Hazel nudges me, and her eyes widen as she sees Cameron walking back– with Simon in tow.

My heart begins to race, because what the *fuck* is Simon doing here of all places? I quickly hide my concern as Cameron walks up to us, wrapping his arm around me and smiling wide.

"Look who I found! I figured the more the merrier for the room. Hope you guys don't mind, plus you remember Simon, right?" Cameron gives me a gentle squeeze and this imperceptive emotion flashes over Simon's face that goes unnoticed by everyone but me.

"T-thanks Cameron. What a c-coincidence running into you guys here. D-Detective A-Alex had me scouting out some p-places for the youth p-program. I-I had no i-idea you were going t-to b-be here," Simon stutters out as he gives an unsettling smile. I don't know what it is, but the vibes that come off of him make me so uncomfortable. Hazel, on the other hand, being her happy-go-lucky self, smiles and nods.

"Fuck yea! Let's go break some shit!" Hazel shouts overexcitedly.

We don't really get more than a moment to react to Simon joining our group and then the teenage worker walks up to us, giving the orientation spiel. After going over the introduction and rules, he leads us to the room we're going to be in for the next hour. He hands us the PPE, a gown, and safety glasses. We're then shown a wall of tools that we can use; there are sledgehammers, baseball bats, golf clubs, wrenches, and more. I can't help but smile as we all grab our tools and the timer starts.

There's a bunch of tables, computers, and plates lining a fake living room and kitchen. Unexpectedly, flashes of my past bubble to the surface just at the sheer impression of these rooms accompanied with the sensation of impending violence. I try my best to push them out of my mind— not here, not now. The four of us get the okay to begin, and we all just stand around at first, not really wanting to be the one to start. Cameron smiles wickedly, a gleam in his eyes as our gazes connect.

"Are we just gonna stand here?" Hazel teases, breaking the silence. Her eyes are bright as she continues, walking over to the kitchen set up. With flourish, she picks up a plate and screams as she chucks it against the wall. And I mean really *screams*. As if it had been her thrown against that wall and shattered into pieces upon impact. It makes my heart ache as I realize even though she stays far more composed than me, Hazel probably needs this outlet just as much.

"That's for the man who killed my dad." Her chest heaves with heavy breaths, and she looks at us with eyes that gleam with relief. And suddenly, the rest of us are eager to join in.

Simon grins and takes his bat to an old computer, "T-This is for t-the b-bitch who cheated on m-me!"

I smirk as I take the sledgehammer to the coffee pot on the counter. "For the person who keeps leaving me flowers!" I swing with all my might and let out a laugh as the thing goes flying. All hell breaks out as the four of us start throwing and breaking the things around the room.

There's not much speaking, just grunts and screams as the hour passes by. I turn to Cameron who's going to town on a table, he's got this look in his eyes that almost scares me. He's yelling as he yields a metal baseball bat that has a hollow *thud* with every blow. The words go unheard, but I realize he's not really here right now. That's what that look is— he's in another place and another time. And that table isn't just some table in a junk room. It's a table somewhere in his memory.

My heart wrenches seeing the look on his face, I just know he's seeing someone– and I probably know who. His dad might be dead, but he's still got Cameron in his deadly grasp. The other two are staring now, and the room gone completely still other than Cameron and that bat.

"I got this..." I whisper, as Haze and Simon look at me with concern, and I give a soft smile. They know his story, they know what Cameron went through, there's no judgement in their eyes as they nod in acknowledgment.

He's helped me so much, and now is the time to return the favor.

I slowly walk towards him. That thousand yard stare is still dominating his face and his voice is growing hoarse even though he continues to scream. "Cam–" my voice is gentle but loud. "Cameron, look at me."

When he doesn't, I take a few more steps towards him in hopes of gaining his attention. I need to get him out of whatever hell he's in right now, that way we can work to calm him back down.

His head snaps up to me, and he bares his teeth, an almost animalistic growl escapes his lips. "Baby– look at me, you're not there– you–" I don't even have a moment to react, his hand is around my throat as I'm shoved against the wall.

"Cameron!" Simon yells charging towards me, but I'm warding them off.

"No—No, it's okay... I've got this." My hands wrap around Cameron's wrist, his hand presses my throat but not enough to cause any pain. His eyes are almost unseeing looking past the present moment, a gleam in them, but I'm not scared.

Cameron's chest heaves as he doesn't move off of me, my voice is confident and steady. "Cameron, baby– it's not real. Your dad is dead. Your dad isn't here. He can't hurt you anymore." His eyes connect with mine, as his hand tightens ever so slightly, his breaths slowly starting to calm. "Good, come back to me Cameron, come back to your Cherry. This isn't you, this isn't *you*."

I emphasize the last word, hoping to get through to him that I know my Cameron wouldn't do this. This is something that his father has caused to be alive in him, but it doesn't mean that *this* is who he is.

I'm gently rubbing the back of his wrist with my fingers, as I keep repeating that mantra back to him, when I feel it. His fingers slightly loosen and I can sense the warmth returning to him. "There you are," I whisper as I see the light slowly fill Cameron's eyes again. They instantly widen and his hand releases my throat as he backs away quickly.

"Leyla, I-I'm so sorry..." He whispers as he looks at the three of us in the room, his eyes roving over us as he realizes what he's just done.

"Cameron, it's okay– you're oka–"

"*No*," Cameron interrupts, as he looks around once more. "I'm so sorry– I–" And then, he runs out of the room. I hurry after him, but by the time I get out to the lobby, he's out the door and speeding away.

I walk back inside, finding Hazel and Simon talking in hushed tones to each other, their eyes connecting with mine when I close in on them. "He– He left…" I whisper, sounding almost defeated. Shit, I guess I am defeated— defeated that I couldn't help him the way he's helped me so many times before.

"I can drive you guys home," Simon offers— a little too quickly for my liking. Maybe I'm being judgmental, but I swear he sounds rather chipper considering what just occurred.

I look at Hazel, and she sighs, knowing we really don't have an option. "That would be great," Hazel replies begrudgingly. I want to scream *no* at the top of my lungs, grab Hazel's hand and run away; my childhood didn't teach me much but I at least paid attention to the after-school programs enough to not get in a car with a stranger. But, we're trapped forty-five minutes away from Maplewood, so this is our best option aside from rideshare. And I suppose that is getting in a car with a stranger, and at least this one we vaguely know.

And yet, there's a knot in my stomach that just won't loosen. Something in me is begging me not to go with Simon, even if he seemed harmless. "We can call a car, really. It's no problem! I don't wanna put you out," I try to offer.

"No, really, it's f-fine. I don't mind. We all live there anyway. Maplewood, I mean," Simon insists almost nervously as he puts on his awkward smile.

I look at Hazel and shrug. "Yea, let's go." I relent.

The three of us make our way to his truck. The ride home is

quiet, and I'm honestly grateful for that. I text Cameron, needing him to know that I'm here and that if he needs anything to call me. Subconsciously, I run my hand over my neck, I can't tell if it's hot from everything I'm feeling or if Cameron left a mark. Hazel scoots toward me, linking our arms and pulling me close.

"You okay?" she asks, her voice barely above a whisper.

I fight back the tears that threaten to fall and open my mouth before snapping it shut, truly not knowing how or what to feel right now. I nod weakly, though I don't believe it even as I confirm.

A nervous energy is building in my stomach, worried that if I don't smooth this over with Hazel, she would hate him forever— or worse. And I don't want my best friend and my— my what? boyfriend seems too eager— *my Cameron* to be at odds.

Words are falling out of my mouth with little thought, and I pray I can at least string together something mildly coherent. "I'm mad at him, but also I just want to make sure he's okay. He would never hurt me, he's not like that. I hope you believe me when I say that." My voice is hoarse as I look at her. "Are you staying?" My eyes pleading and she frowns.

Hazel reluctantly informs me, "This was a one-day thing, babes. My plane leaves from Traverse City at 8:30."

I can't help but pout now that I know this isn't going to be an all weekend thing. Of course I know she has her own life to get back to, but selfishly, I had hoped she would stay after what all just happened. My emotions are running rampant right now; I catch Simon's eyes in the rear view, but he quickly looks away acting as if he wasn't just fully listening to our entire conversation.

Unaware, Hazel smiles and kisses my cheek. "LeyLey, you've got me for four more hours, and we will make the most of it. We will cuddle, watch *The Princess Bride*, and pretend all of this never happened, okay?"

I nod— that honestly sounds perfect and just what I need with my best friend. Simon drives us home, the rest of the way is silent, and music plays quietly in the background.

We pull up to my apartment, and I try to remember if I had given him my address or just told him the complex. Had I said anything? I can't remember, my mind is such a mess right now.

Simon gets out of the car and opens the door for Hazel and me. When I step out onto the sidewalk, he takes an uncomfortably close step toward me. I glance his way to see his face flushed and his hand rubbing the back of his neck. He stammers, "I-If you ever want to g-go on a d-date or something, I'm h-here... waiting... any t-time."

I don't have the heart to tell him it will never happen, but I nod and start pulling Hazel toward the building. "Thanks for the ride home. We appreciate it." Before he even has a chance to respond, I hurry Hazel along and run inside.

Hazel turns to me as we walk into the apartment. "C'mon. Bed, *now*." She grabs my hand and I am once again reminded that no matter what happens, she's my constant— and I am so fucking thankful that I have her.

"I love you, Haze," I whisper as I get my door unlocked.

"I love you too, Leyley." She smiles back, squeezing my hand tight. "Now, let's go. Dread Pirate Roberts is calling our names."

I can't help but laugh as we head to the bedroom and talk and spend time until her rideshare comes to pick her up hours later.

When she's gone, I pull out my phone and text Cameron. I haven't heard from him since this afternoon, and even though my mind is still unorganized and conflicted, I'm worried about him.

17
MISTAKES MADE
CAMERON

The thoughts that spiraled around in my head were all so fucking loud and it wouldn't stop.

I hurt her. The one thing I swore to never do was hurt her, and I did it. The pain that sits in the base of my spine, crawling up from how tense my shoulders are. The thoughts want to do terrible things, and I have to constantly remind myself that I'm not him. I'm *not* my father.

The day is undone by a single moment that flashed in my memories, and the self-doubt and my fucking father's words echoed in the forefront of my mind. In that room, I hadn't been a twenty-six year old man, I was that twelve year old kid again, being beaten with a belt for not coming home on time. I could smell the whiskey on his breath like I was there. *Like he was there.*

The horrible truth was painfully simple: I had wanted to

hurt her. And that makes me a fucking monster, just like my dad. The flashbacks threaten to come back as I drive aimlessly, but I can't let them.

No– NO.

I switch gears in the car and take off at a breakneck speed hoping and praying that there isn't a cop hiding nearby, that's the last thing I need right now. I just know I need to get away, and I need to do it fast.

"You fucking idiot, useless–*fucking useless!*"

I hit my steering wheel hard, hitting it over and over again until my hands are stinging with pain.

FUCK. Fuck. fuck. FU– **no.**

That word echoes around in my psyche as I finally regain some semblance of a normal breathing pattern and flashes of today play back in my mind. How did I fuck it up so badly when it was going so fucking well?

I should know better that I'll never deserve someone as good and pure as her. Someone who when she looks at me doesn't look at me like I'm this fucking broken thing of a man. She sees me for me, not the child of a monster. I found her again, I fucking found her and I lost her all in one fucking day. My phone buzzes with a message from her, and I ignore it.

I don't deserve her.

I keep driving, not stopping until I finally get my breathing down to a safe level. Skidding to a stop on the shoulder of the road, I fling my door open and fall to my knees on the gravel.

How is it that someone who is dead still has such a hold over my soul and all the broken parts of me that he caused?

That *he* broke? My chest feels as though it could collapse in on itself with the force of a supernova. Why did I have to turn out like this? Why can't I just forget everything and just move on? I want to place my childhood in a box and ditch it deep in the countryside so that even if it got loose, there would be no one around for it to hurt.

But I hurt, as much as I want to deny it and lock it away, I do. And I hurt people— worst of all, I hurt *her*.

I have to get ahold of myself. This is my mess, but I'm not going to let one fucking moment ruin what I've been building with Leyla. I will get her back. I'll prove to her that I'm worthy of her.

I take a breath and stand up, brushing the dirt off my pants. I pull out my phone and call the man who has always helped keep me grounded and has done too many favors for me to count— Zack, my best friend. And as if on cue, he picks up after one ring.

"Cam? The fucks wrong?" His voice is raspy, it's clear he is busy, but he always makes the time for me. I'm silent for a moment, trying to figure out what the fuck I say. "Cameron?" Zack says a bit louder, trying to wrap my attention back to him.

"I lost it, Zack," I finally squeak out. "I lost it on her. On *her*." I clear my throat in hopes that it will clear the pressure that's been building up in it. "We were on a fucking group date, and I had a flashback— I-I... I choked her, Z." The guilt is present in my voice as I take a deep breath. "What do I do?" I feel the pressure growing in my chest again, as I place my hand on my heart.

"I thought you... had it under control?" Zack's voice is vague and unfeeling, just like the bastard always is. And yet, he somehow always knows what to do or say to keep my feet on the ground.

I begin pacing as I try to keep my breathing steady. "I did. I had... had... therapy last week." I try to get out, trying to get my hands to keep from shaking; I keep my voice as strong as I can, doing my best not to stutter.

What the fuck is wrong with me? This isn't me. This isn't what I do or how I act— just like Leyla had tried to say to me.

"You need to talk to her, Cam. Tell her the fucking truth because you're gonna drive yourself crazy if you don't. You know what you do and what you're like. Don't fucking come to me crying cause you are scared of what you've done. 'Cause that doesn't change who you are. If she's anything like you've told me, you better be honest with her 'cause she ain't stupid." His voice is solid, and his Tennessee twang makes him seem wise beyond his years.

I know that I have to listen to him, he's not wrong. I'm just scared that I'm going to lose everything the moment I set the truth free.

"You're right... You're right." The confidence grows in my voice when I repeat the words, as the world isn't moving as fast and isn't as loud.

"Yea, I know. Gotta go, Cam. Talk to her. Text me later." I don't even get to say goodbye as he hangs up on me and I let out a sigh. I guess it's time to be honest with her about my past.

Making my way back to the car, I pull my phone out and read her message. I will tell her the truth about me, just... not today. I've done enough damage for one day. I'll let her have those last few hours with her friend before she had to catch her flight, and some time to handle what she just went through. Right now, I doubt she needs me begging for forgiveness like some fool.

I don't deserve her, but I still want her.

Putting my car in drive I blast some *Bad Omens* and head back to the safety of Maplewood.

18

CHERRY

LEYLA

Cameron hasn't texted me back since our meet up with Hazel and Simon. It's to the point I'm getting kind of worried. I texted Zack, as Cameron had given me his number in case of emergency and this is starting to feel like one. I ask if he has heard anything from Cam, my hands shaking viciously as I do; and I just stare at the text thread after it's sent, willing him to respond right away.

Today just feels *wrong* and I can't quite pinpoint why. I dig around in my drawer, pulling out my pocketknife that I used to keep on me at all times. It's pink with a long switchblade and has *LeyLey* etched into the plastic handle— a gift from Hazel in high school. As she said 'every bad bitch needs her own weapon'.

Why had I stopped carrying it? I don't know, but I know it makes for a good fidget because of the easy-press latch. I carry it around with me as I wait for Zack to respond, needing some sort of outlet for the nervous energy that's building up in me.

Looking at myself in the mirror in the bathroom when my anxious pacing takes me here, I feel *weird.* Like I'm not attached to the person that I'm looking at. Quickly, I splash some cold water on my face in hopes that maybe it'll shock my system to center again. The nerves that I'm feeling threaten to overwhelm me and I don't know what else to do. I press call on my phone, and, not even a moment later, Alex is on the phone.

"Hey sweetheart, what's wrong?" Alex asks me, her motherly instincts so clear and comforting. I immediately feel better hearing her voice. Something familiar and grounding.

"I know this is super last minute, but do you have time to grab lunch?" my voice belaying the nerves that are consuming me whole. I need to tell her what's been going on, and I need to do it now. I've officially hit my limit and I know that if I don't get something out, I'll explode. *Or implode.* "I know you're super busy, but– actually, never mind– it's dumb... I'm just overreacting."

Alex interrupts me, "Meet me at Harvey's Diner in twenty? I told you, I'll always make time for you." Relief floods my veins, taking the edge off my impending mental breakdown; like Tylenol to a migraine.

I release a slow breath and nod although she can't see me, quickly responding in the affirmative. "Y-Yea. Harvey's Diner. See you soon." She says her goodbyes and I head off towards Harvey's, as quickly as I can.

———

Making my way through the downtown area of Maplewood, I walk with purpose and make it to the diner in what has to be record time. As soon as I step inside, I see Detective Alexandra already waiting for me, her dusty brown hair clipped into a short pixie. Waving, I make my way over and she's up and wrapping her arms around me tight.

My face can't hide the utter fear and worry that's been consuming me whole, as her smile falls and concern creases the space between her brows. She moves me to sit down in the booth, her sitting on the same side as me. "Leyla, what's going on? You can tell me anything."

So, I do. I tell Alex everything that's been happening. From the roses that I'd been receiving to the funeral arrangement in my apartment, Cameron, the visit with Hazel, and I even tell her about the reuniting with Simon too. Her face portrays nothing as she lets me get everything out.

"And now Cameron's not responding to me, and I know that's the least of my problems... I can't help but feel that somehow he realized it was all too much, and I was too much for him."

Alexandra gently grabs my hands and squeezes them. "I'm sure he just needs time to decompress. It sounds like that brought back some memories for him that he probably didn't realize he would be reliving so soon. Don't worry yourself sick — give him some time."

Talking all this through makes me feel so much better about the whole situation. With my mind clearing and my focus shifting to the present, I feel it. It's not overt, but I can sense the thickness of the air around Alex. Through all the years of over analyzing everything I know when moods change, I know when people are hiding things.

She's fucking hiding something.

"Why didn't you tell me sooner about the flowers, Ley?"

I want to focus on the flowers and maybe get some semblance of an idea of what could be going on with all that, but I can't seem to let go of the feeling that she's hiding something. Annoyance and anxiety spikes in me.

Alex looks concerned when I don't reply. I watch as she waits for a moment longer, as if hoping I'll say more, before relenting.

"Leyla," Alex starts, clearing her throat. There's something more to her tone now, and I have a feeling that she's going to say what she's hiding from me. Maybe my silence told her everything I needed to say; that I'm not saying shit until she says whatever is on her mind. But the darkness in her eyes and the way her mouth twitches... My nerves are hitting me harder than expected.

She starts again, "The Whispering Killer has been active again. Five people in the past three months. They're so organized and they leave nothing behind. Leyla, I'm not supposed to say anything, I wasn't going to tell you until we had more to go off of... But with these flowers and everything? Something doesn't feel right to me, and I think you should know now."

I sit there in silence again, my chest ready to explode and I don't even know where to begin processing that information. I thought this was all behind me— that I was free and clear from this. But maybe this is my punishment for some crime in a past life that I could never atone for; I would never be free from those horrors, they would follow me around for the rest of my life.

"Sweetheart. I promise you, you're safe. We are doing everything in our power to find out who this is."

I can see the concern in her eyes, but I can't handle this right now. The words don't register, but she's still talking, "– but we have reason to believe it's tied to Cameron— Hey, Leyla –" but I'm already on my feet.

I'm too reactive today and I feel it, even as I find myself storming away without a word. My blood is instantly at a boil with Cameron's name in her mouth over my parents. My parents. *My fucking parents.* How could she do this? Why would she listen to me talk about how wonderful Cameron is and how I'm so worried things are ruined right now, and then implicate him in a serial killer plot that resulted in *my parents being murdered?*

Maybe she's lost her mind. After all, Cameron was what? *Twelve* when my parents were murdered? Something about the thought makes the back of my head... tingle. Tingle might not be the right word, but it feels as if something is buzzing in the back of my head that's cold and uncomfortable. It's all I can focus on as I head down the sidewalk without purpose or direction.

Cameron was twelve when my parents were killed. That means he was way too young to be involved. The killer is active again, though. What was that with his trunk? Cameron was twelve when my parents were killed. No one that young could be a meticulous killer. He was twelve. That's so young to be involved in something so dark.

My thoughts won't stop and I feel myself nearing the edge of sanity. Not paying attention to anything else around me, I know that I have to get home, I need to call him.

Running faster than I ever have before, the buildings a blur of color next to me, I make it to the back of my apartment building. Pulling out my phone I dial Cameron, just hoping that he would answer, there's nothing else I need in this world right now except to talk to Cameron Curtis.

"Cherry," Cameron answers with a sigh. "I'm so sorry—Fuck, that doesn't even begin to cover what I did. And I'm bad with this shit, and I know I'm even more of an ass for hiding like—"

"Did you kill my parents?" The question slips out before I even have time to process what I'm thinking, implying, or *anything*. My brain just won't *stop*. It's a record on loop, stuck on thinking about how young Cameron would have been when my parents were killed. *Why?* There has to be a reason that my mind won't let it go. Fuck, I should have heard Alex out, but I just... couldn't handle it. I can't handle any of this shit.

My hand is clutching the phone tightly, and my breathing is more like panting. But I persist, "Don't even *think* about lying to me."

I say looking around the parking lot in the back of my building. I already know the answer as a barrage of memories flood back to me, rendering me speechless. There's not even time for me to hear Cameron's response, as suddenly the world around me fades to black.

19
KNOWING ME, KNOWING YOU
CAMERON

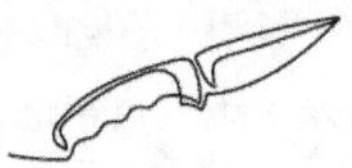

"*D*ad— *please no. Please, don't make me watch this,*" my little voice is barely above a whisper as my dad shoves me back into the wall, telling me to shut up or I'll get it. I won't make a sound. I know better than that.

I watch my dad grab the woman's hair and cut her throat. Blood is everywhere and I want to look away, but I know he'll get mad. My dad always told me it's for my own good. That one day I'll follow in his footsteps. I just want to make him proud.

Unable to take in that much red, I dare to look away for just a second; I just need a moment to steel myself. And that's when I see another flash of red. That's when I see her. *A little girl with red hair is running from one room to another, I can see it through the crack in the door that looks down the hallway. I don't tell dad. I won't tell dad.*

I will protect her, that's my job now. Because I know if dad finds out there's a loose end… well, there won't be one. I'll protect her from all this mayhem. Somehow, I will.

I turn back to my dad as he puts the woman back on the bed. Her blue eyes are looking at me— but not at the same time. The man in the corner is crying as dad makes his way over to him. They're talking loudly. The man says he didn't kill anyone, but my dad wouldn't be here if that was the case.

I know what my dad does isn't good, but he always made it clear that he only hurts people who deserve it. Dad calls me over to him, his rough hand on the small of my back, and he places the knife in my hand.

"One movement. Make it count, kid," Dad says to me with a too wide grin. "You are a killer at heart, just like me okay? You know who I am, and you are going to be just like me when you grow up. Get that? Don't fucking let me down." Dad's voice grows louder, as he grabs my arm and drags me into the hallway right outside the room. Immediately my eyes dart around to see if the red-headed girl is still in sight. I don't see her— good.

Dad towers over me as he coaches me once again on what to do. Shame fills my stomach as I can't help but feel special when he's talking to me like this. His voice is a little lower and I swear, a little softer as he mimes how to cut and to hold my chest up high with pride. I shouldn't like this—but this also shouldn't be the only sort of love I feel from him.

"I'll be back, he better be fucking dead when I get back," he commands. I swallow hard as I nod. I can't let him down— if I don't do this, he's gonna hurt me again. He always hurts me.

I take a breath and step back into the room, clutching the weapon. But, I stop dead in my tracks as soon as the door is closed behind me. The red-haired little girl stands there next to her dead-eyed father.

She... she killed him.

Her little hands stand there shaking, with one of dad's knives in her hand. She stands there in shock as I walk over to her taking the knife out of her hand. "Go... Y-you need to go!" I whisper yell at the little girl. She's not listening to me, and I dig deep to find the sort of command that my dad always has. "Did you fucking hear me, kid?! GO!"

She probably has no idea what she's done— she seems to be in shock, as there's nothing on her face as her body trembles like she's cold. I grab her arm and shove her in the closet and tell her to stay put.

She will truly never know what she's done for me today. She saved me from my first kill, something I'm not ready for. Even though she's littler than me and seems to be terrified, she's stronger than me. Maybe stronger than I'll ever be.

But for her, I'll learn to be strong. I'll have to, to protect her from my bastard of a father.

I quickly place my hand around the handle of dad's knife and slice it across the man's neck again, so that he'll believe me.

Maybe this once things will be different. What was so bad that she killed him herself?

———

The memories of that night hit me like a semi-truck. My body shakes with a rage that I probably shouldn't be feeling. I can't let her figure this out. I never thought it would be so soon for us to take *this* trip down memory lane. I have to get to her. I have to run to her, I have to fix this. She is mine to protect. Her terrified words hit me again as they echo in my mind: *"Don't even think about lying to me."*

I'm already driving to her apartment; I had headed that way even before she had called. I had planned to make her dinner, if she would even let me in after what happened in the rage room. But fuck the steaks in my passenger seat. This is... huge. This is now way more than a PTSD fuck up that needed a lifetime of perfect behavior to make up for.

In that moment I decide on what I have to do, she will always be mine to protect, and my answer will be her reason for being okay again. We can explore her past together, but my answer isn't a total lie, but it's not the whole truth either.

"Yes."

The answer falls on deaf ears as I step out of my car into the empty back parking lot of her apartment.

PART TWO

20
PLEASE, PLEASE, PLEASE
LEYLA

My head is fucking *throbbing*.

It's dark and it's clear that I'm tied up from the rough material around my wrists and lack of mobility I now have. I groan as I try to wiggle my hands, trying to get out of the tight restraints. I can't see much of anything, but it seems like I'm in some sort of storage unit from the tall gray walls and echoey sounds that you only hear in places like this. I crane my neck trying to see if there's anything, any sort of window or anything that could give me any ideas as to where I am.

Nothing. Can anyone hear me? The thoughts come racing through my mind, and the tears burning behind my eyes, there's no chance of me getting out of this this time. I already escaped death once in my life and I feel like my quota has been met. My head hangs low as tears fall down my cheeks, a sob wracks my body. I shoot up when I hear the clanging of a key. I close my eyes as light assaults them. I turn away to get out of the line of it.

"Well, well, well," a modulated voice emerges from the darkness that once again covers the room. My hands constantly move as I attempt to get out of the restraints that are holding me down. "You think you're so clever, and so fucking smart. Yet, clearly you need a little reminder of who you are."

I squint my eyes in the hope that I'll be able to see something, when suddenly a masked man is standing in front of me, the look in his eyes unhinged and dangerous. I don't know what to do. If I could just get my hands untied, then I can grab the knife that I know I tucked away in my pocket, the damn restraints just aren't budging.

My heart is beating out of my chest, but I don't let my face portray anything. "It's pretty pathetic that you think you have to tie me up to talk to me."

The portrait of calm settles over me, as I keep moving my wrists, feeling the rope start to give ever so slightly. I don't know how I'm managing to keep my shit together so well. Maybe because there's nothing else for me now but my life.

It's Cameron, it has to be. But I'll play dumb, I'll play his stupid little game. The figure stalks around me and I know he's stalling. I don't quite know where this unfettered courage comes from, especially since I'm in no position to be testing the waters.

"Come on, Cameron. Really— this some sort of fucked up fantasy for you? You gonna kill me too?" I watch the figure's posture stiffen as he whirls to me.

"Cameron? FUCKING CAMERON CURTIS?!" the voice speaks

above the voice modulator, the distortion pitching and breaking as it attempts to keep up. "You're so fucking in love with that man, but he doesn't deserve you! He's *never* deserved you!" the man screams out as he rips off his mask.

The crazed look in his eye as he storms towards me has pinned me in place, my mind not processing anything anymore. As if those eyes have CTRL+ALT+DEL and ends any task that attempts to load in my brain.

It's not Cameron.

"Simon." My breath hitches in my throat as he grabs my chin forcefully. Pulling his face into mine, he kisses me. I fight back as much as I can, thrashing my body around to no avail. I don't want to feel his lips on mine or feel his breath on my skin. I want this moment to *end.*

He pulls away, his eyes so wide and round that the entirety of his irises are visible. "Don't you know how good we could be together, Leyla? How perfect would we be together?! Don't you like the presents I leave you?!"

He sounds insane, the timbre of his voice cracking with every word he speaks.

I close my eyes and turn my head away as I try to keep calm as his screams reverberate off the walls. "I AM SO MUCH BETTER THAN HIM! DON'T YOU KNOW I'VE LOVED YOU SINCE WE WERE KIDS?!"

My ears *ache* from the volume and my heart thuds as each word registers to my mind. He's been in love with me? He's the one leaving the flowers? But I can't harbor on that. I'm watching Simon come apart at his seams, panting and shaking as he paces around. Then, he snaps back in my direction and his hand darts to my throat.

"He doesn't deserve you. He's weak, *pathetic*." His hand is like a vice around my throat, as he forces his lips onto me again. I close my eyes not wanting to see this, begging for any cosmic power to make this stop.

"Mmmm. You taste amazing," he growls, the insecurity dripping from his words. He holds my chin in place, forcing me to meet his eyes which are narrowed now, his lips twitching into a sick smile. "Does he taste as good as I do? I don't think I've ever tasted something so sweet, my Cherry."

My stomach drops at the use of my nickname— one only Cameron calls me. Even though all I should be feeling is sheer terror, anger strikes through me like lightning. The fucking *nerve* of him to use a nickname so fucking special to me after calling Cameron pathetic. It makes me want to actually *hurt* him.

"Fuck– fuck you," I grit out. Might as well go out swinging if I'm going to die here. "I would never fucking date you! I would *never* be with you! You aren't half the man Cameron is! You don't even compare! You're insane!"

My outburst causes me to thrash— and I feel it then, the knot is undone. I can't help but feel a momentary pang for Cameron, even now I'm drawing strength from him. It takes so much focus to control my face so that my shock doesn't show in the midst of all this fury. He needs to stay completely oblivious. Even though I slip out of the poorly tied rope, I hold my hands steady. I can't let him see, I just need to wait for the right moment.

"You *stupid* slut!" Simon hisses.

Then, I'm struck on the back of the head. I try to fight the dull but consuming pain, but black spots are forming in my vision from the blow and whatever the hell he did to me to get me to his lair. God, I fucked up. I don't know why I get so reactive about Cameron, but I just... lost it. And now I need to make up with the crazy man to have any chance of getting out of here alive.

"Simon, please. I-I don't understand!" I plead, though I think I'm just talking to try and stay conscious.

I feel myself losing both battles: appealing to the humanity in Simon, and holding onto consciousness. The look in his eyes is empty and cold and his face is all I can see. The rage etched into the fine lines of his face, the sweat beading on his forehead.

"I told you to shut the fuck up!" Simon screeches. He knocks me in the back of my head once again and the black dots overtake my vision.

21

WHAT THE FUCK?

CAMERON

As I step out of my car, I hear tires squealing and my heart drops to something lower than my stomach— Hell perhaps. I look at my phone, seeing the ongoing call and hearing my own footsteps echoing through the speakers.

"Leyla?!" I holler into the too quiet night.

My heart races as I run around the parking lot, coming across the skidding tire marks and her phone lying on the ground, our call still ongoing and my screams and bounding footsteps helping me find it.

Rage bubbles up in my throat and I let out an animalistic growl. Closing my eyes to desperately hold onto my center so I don't totally lose myself to the madness I know lingers inside of me, I pick up Leyla's phone, put it in my pocket, and immediately call Zack.

"Z, we have a problem," my voice unnaturally even for the hurricane brewing in my head.

There's silence on the other end, but I know that he's listening. I immediately go into logic mode as I hop back in the Maserati. "I had you looking into her past regarding the stalker. Any status update on that?"

Zack's low voice finally answers, sounding a bit bored, "Nothing out of the ordinary. You already know everything about her father. The cemetery that he buried his victims in has been excavated. There are no children of his victims that would be targeting her. Her best friend checks out. The overbearing mother-figure detective as well. She has no contact with her adoptive or foster families." He lists off all the finalized results that he's gathered so far. He's a fairly decent hacker, so he's got his hands in places that most people don't have access to.

"Zack, someone took her." My voice belies the fear and anxiety that is racing through me and barely contained by my forced composure that I trained all my life to master. *Thanks, dad.*

"What do you mean someone *took* her?" Zack huffs in disbelief. When his comment isn't followed up by anything to let him know I'm being dramatic, he speaks again. "Cameron, we will find her."

"If something happens to her, Z, I promise you, I will stop at nothing to fucking kill everyone who played a hand in this. *Everyone.*" My voice is cold and emotionless. "I should never have left her, Zack. I never should have ran away from her. She should have never left my sight."

I can hear him rummaging around and hard taps of a

keyboard. "I'm pulling up the cameras around her complex. I got your location. Give me twenty minutes to comb through what I've got," Zack confirms.

If there's anyone who can help me find her, it's Zack.

I turn the car on and start driving towards my storage unit. It seems I'm going to be needing some tools to help me find my girl— and kill the son of a bitch who's trying to take her away from me.

I speak into the emptiness that is my car, almost like a prayer. "I'm coming, Cherry. I will find you."

22
NO NOTES
LEYLA

I groan as I come to, blinking my eyes. I don't know what to expect around me. Thankfully for me, and stupidly on his part, he didn't notice that my arms had gotten loose from the restraints. They are still in the ropes, but they are loose enough to easily maneuver. Alright, my progress hasn't been undone— time to figure out what's next. My head hurts like a bitch, so when I move to look around, I move slowly so as to not irritate it anymore.

"Well, well, you're awake again." Simon's irritating voice echoes in the room and I can't suppress the shudder that racks my body.

"What do you want from me, Simon?" I hoarsely reply. I'm going to have to play his little game. All I want is to not be here with this creep of a man, and being in Cameron's arms would be pretty sweet, too.

He scoffs as if I've said something utterly ridiculous. "I want you, Leyla. Like I told you already— I have always wanted you! I love you even when you never saw me!"

Simon's eyes burn with a hunger that even Bundy couldn't replicate. I've never seen Simon in that light, the light he wants me to. And I honestly have no idea what he means by *'I never saw him'*. Did he mean in group? I don't even remember group, I barely remember anything before high school thanks to my mind locking it up and throwing away the key.

He's looking at me expectantly, as if waiting for me to burst into tears and confess to countless times of turning my nose up at him. And the more moments that pass that I don't, the deeper the anger sets in on his face.

I'm blurting out anything that comes to mind. "Simon, I'm sorry, okay? I was just a kid when we met! You expect me to remember all the way back then?" My voice betrays me, I try to sound confident but there's a tremor in it that I try to force down.

"You're *sorry?*" Simon growls as he prowls towards me, his hand gently caresses my cheek. I yank my head away but he grabs my chin, forcing me to look at him.

"Simon, please, *please* don't hurt me." My confidence is quickly waning and I'm certain that I won't be able to get out of this alive. I'm going to die in this fucking storage room by a man who's apparently loved me since we were kids and is pissed off that I've been blowing him off all this time when I hardly remembered his existence. I close my eyes as his grip on my chin tightens.

"I won't hurt you. No, no. Cherry, baby," Simon purrs. Every ounce of malice is gone from his voice, and he is practically cooing at me. "I'm just going to make sure you know how much I love you! I'm going to show you what you've been missing out on. Simon and Leyla forever... and ever... and ever." he trails off as he suddenly snaps his gaze toward me.

I don't want this, fuck knows I don't need this happening to me, and I don't know what I'm going to do.

"You love me?" I hear myself say, though I feel disconnected from my mouth.

I need to play his game, I remind myself. "If you love me so much Simon, can you do me a favor?" My voice is saccharine sweet knowing that I can get anything I want from him. I've known people like him before.

"Anything for you, Leyla. What do you need?" his voice betrays the look in his eyes. His thoughts seem scattered and his movements jittery with excitement. "I knew you'd see things my way, because of course I love you Leyla. I knew you'd see past that scum of a man *Cameron*." He spits out Cam's name like it's painful for him.

"I need some water, please?" I look at him through hooded eyes, his face brightens as he nods. "Maybe some food? I haven't eaten all day and if you want me to be yours, you've gotta keep me alive. Can you do that for me? I know that you're so big and strong, but I really need you to be my hero and get me something to eat, okay?"

Simon nods like a bobblehead, and gently kisses my cheek, as he caresses the other with a trembling hand. "Anything for you, my love." The words and the touch burn me, but I make no movement. I show no reaction to him.

"Thank you, honey. I'll be here." I put a smile on my face,

knowing that he's falling for my performance. He's so desperate to hear what he's been waiting all these years for, that it only takes an inkling for him to latch on.

Without any more hesitation, he turns and hurries for the exit, muttering to himself as he debated what he should get me to eat. I can't help but keep that smile on my face, quite pleased with myself— that is, until I hear the three locks clicking into place as he walks out and traps me in this room. When I hear a car pulling away, a sigh of relief escapes me. My shoulders sag as I finally let myself cry, again. I can't do this.

I quickly pull my hands out of the ropes and pull the knife out of my shoe, and finally begin cutting the ropes that were around my ankles. My hands shake nervously as I finally get free of all the bindings and stand up. The blood rushes to my head and I sway with the pain that is rushing through my body. I need to get out of here.

Wherever *here* is...

As soon as I get my bearings, I start running around the room, banging on the door and walls screaming, just hoping that there's someone, anyone around. I press my ear to the door and there's nothing. There's not a single sound that I can hear.

My heart sinks as I realize there's nothing I can fucking do. I take a deep breath and sigh, sinking to the ground, pocketknife in my hand while I hang my head into my hands.

"Cameron... Please, find me." I whisper as my sobbing overtakes me.

23
METAL DOORS
CAMERON

I speed down 5th street, the downtown buildings morphing into a color-speckled blur as I make my way towards my storage unit. I'm certain that Zack will find something— he *has* to. I've gotta make this right, explain every-thing to her, and I make the internal promise to myself to fix this no matter the cost. Even if it means she will hate me.

I had no choice back then, and I had no idea what she would become to me. I might have swore to myself to protect always all those years ago, but I never thought it would ever be more than keeping a watchful eye on her from a distance. I may have wanted to marry her from the moment I saw her at group, but it had been a boy's pining dream. A little fantasy to escape into when my days were too dark to bear. I never thought it would turn into this.

Though, I suppose that our pasts are too similar and too

interwoven for us to be around one another in any capacity and not fall into this fucked up web that I've made for us.

My knuckles are so white on the steering wheel, I start to think that the skin would rip. How did this get so far away from me? Why did we *have* to end up like this? Couldn't we have been two normal kids with normal families that fell in love?

No. *Normal* had never been in my fate, nor hers. My dad knew of her father, and her father alone, had taken her to his burial ground many times. I spent so much time reading into the man that was Richard Clarkson, part of me even wonders if she remembers anything from her childhood of who and what her father did.

My phone rings as I answer without even looking at the ID. "Leyla?!"

"It's not Leyla, but I've got an idea of where she might be," Zack's dull voice echoes through the phone speaker.

"Where is she?" I frown, a bite to my voice, as I pull into the parking lot. Throwing the car in park, I run inside the abandoned storage lot.

"You're not gonna like what I'm about to tell you. I need you to stop moving around and think about it for a sec. With your head, not your fucking cock."

I freeze as I hear Zack's words, holding my breath as I look to the door in front of me.

"Who is it, Z?" My voice shakes with fear and the adrenaline comes racing through me. I don't make a single move knowing that my Leyla's life hangs in the balance right now.

She's not cut out for a life like this. Leyla is strong in her own right, but she *needs me;* I want to be the foundation she stands on and the tower that looks out to the horizon to protect her from all. And I need to get to her, to bring her back into the safety of my castle— where no one else will ever enter again.

I start to grow irritated not hearing words come out of his mouth. "Zachary! *Who took my girl?!*" I scream into the phone. I hear him take a breath, annoyance behind that single exhale.

"Simon Maher." Zack's voice shows a hint of fear, contrasting the irritation he had been showing up until this point. Probably because I should have fucking seen this coming a mile away, but I've had my head in the clouds ever since I started getting close to Leyla. "C, you there?"

He's worried about me, I hear it in his voice clearly now. "I've tracked the car that took her to a warehouse probably ten minutes from your current location." I go to interrupt him to ask him to send me the location, but I hear the smirk in his voice. "Already sent it to you, brother. Don't get sloppy over this. You know who you are, and who you're not. Make him fucking pay for what he's done to her, got it? Don't lose yourself over this. You aren't your dad, think logically, and don't do anything I wouldn't do."

Although his last statement doesn't really leave much room for things I could do, I nod though he can't see me, a grin on my face as I enter my pin code into the lock.

"Oh, he's not going to know what fucking hit him. He's going to fucking regret ever touching what's mine. She's mine and he doesn't get to hurt her like that. *Not my girl,*" I growl through gritted teeth.

"Be safe, Cameron. I've got eyes on you now, so you're not alone. Give me the signal and I'll send some of my guys out to you," Zack says as a drone flies over where I'm standing and my eyes widen. I always knew that he was connected, but I really don't know the depth of all that my best friend is truly into. Though, I feel it's probably best that it's kept that way—with me in the dark. I flip off the drone and Zack lets a soft chuckle escape, and I can't help but let one out too. This is why he's my best friend, keeping me grounded to the point of even being able to laugh at my darkest moment.

"I'm gonna take care of this. I'll keep you in the know," I say confidently as I end the call and focus on the task at hand. "I'm coming for you, Cherry."

Leyla is ten minutes from me and the only thing I know for certain is that Simon, while fucking stupid, won't kill her. If he's still in love with her like I suspect him to be, he'll only keep her tied up or locked away. It's the only balm that I've got going for my fucked up little soul right now. The locks click open and the LEDs flick on in my unit.

I make quick work of grabbing everything I need to make sure that Simon Maher never touches my girl ever again. I shake the feeling off of blinding rage and focus back into what I'm doing.

"Knives, chain, taser, scalpel." I pass my finger over the items in my kit that I've rolled open in front of me. I shrug and roll it back up, deciding on the fact I'm going to need it all. He's going to die, one way or another.

———

After an hour of thorough prepping, I've got everything set and ready to go. I pull out my phone and pull up my text thread with Zack.

Zackasaurus Rex: Last seen location: .5 mi from Louis Storage Yard. His white Ranger left the location 15 minutes ago heading eastbound. Just the perp seemed to be leaving. Now's your chance

Cameron: Got it. Keep birds on me. Heading there now. Keep watching for my signal if things go south

Zackasaurus Rex: Affirmative. Be safe

I put my phone away and put the car into gear, the tires squealing as I take off. I'm going to save her, bring her home to me, then I'm going to make Simon pay for taking what's mine.

24
CONTINGENCY
LEYLA

I hide in the corner, and my breath hitches as I hear a car pulling up outside. I can't decide if I want to scream for help and risk it being Simon again— or do I stay here, and go to that place that Daddy once told me to go to? Why am I remembering him right now? Why does my head feel so fucking *fuzzy* every time he comes to mind?

I close my eyes for a moment and open them again with a frown on my face as I look at my tiny pocketknife, my hand gripping the worn metal handle. I know what I have to do. I know what needs to happen.

I stand to the side of the door and hold my breath as I hear the locks jingling. I scrunch my brows, only focusing on what I need to do. It's silent for a moment, but I watch the door as it swings open. Flinging myself in front of the door, I lunge towards the man in the doorway and stab the knife into his left shoulder. The feeling of the blade puncturing flesh makes my stomach flip in a familiar way that makes me dizzier than before. Instantly, there's a pained groan and then the lights flick on.

My eyes connect with the man in front of me: Cameron Curtis. He's standing there, crimson pooling on his white shirt. My eyes widen in shock, and I drop the knife onto the ground.

No. What have I done?!

"Cameron!?" The word escaping my lips doesn't sound like my voice. I'm confused, disconnected, and horrified all at once.

"What–Leyla—*FUCK!*" he groans out as he presses hard on his shoulder where I had stabbed him. I stabbed Cameron, *my* Cameron. My heart is racing and I stand there fully panicking, unsure of what to do.

He closes the distance between us as I'm still frozen in place from the whirlwind of emotions inside me. Cameron grabs my face, looking at me and he's saying something, but I don't hear a single word. I'm fucking horrified. I mumble something unintelligible, but he's just looking me over. He's making sure I'm okay.

He's worrying about me, when I just fucking stabbed him, my boyfriend. No... not boyfriend. I don't think I could honestly tell you what we are at this present moment, because he's the man who killed my parents. I still think I'm in total shock because all I want to do is just be held by him. Just want to be in his arms. I want him– *holy fuck I stabbed him.*

"C-Cam..." I stutter out, as the fog that sits in my head clears ever so slightly. He's looking at me with his emerald eyes and I don't know what to do.

I don't know what's happening.

"I'm here, Cherry. Don't worry, baby girl, you're safe now." Cameron's voice is so clear and calm, I can't help but collapse into his chest.

"S-Si-Sim–" I attempt to get out but it's clear that words are not going to be happening any time soon. Cameron wraps me up in his arms and gently squeezes me into him. It's as if the whole world melts away at that very moment and I don't ever want it to end. I really hope it never does end, honestly.

"I know, baby girl. I know it was Simon, and I promise you, he won't ever hurt you again," Cameron whispers into my bloodied hair. Right, my head is tender still from Simon hitting me. Maybe that's why I'm so confused— but I doubt it. This is all just too fucking much.

"He hurt you?" Cameron's voice is so low it's nearly unrecognizable, his fingers touching the blood. "What did he do? Show me, baby girl; show me where he hurt you."

My whole body is suddenly hit with tremors as the sobs take over. He looks at me, asking again where I am hurt. I don't have it in me to answer, words fail me still. He grabs my chin, forcing me to look at him. His eyes are pitch black right now and I can't tell if it's from pain when I stabbed him, or if it's just from the fact that Cameron Curtis isn't here right now; this man in front of me is the man who killed my parents.

"Baby, he's gonna be back any moment and I know you have no reason to trust me, but I need you to trust me right now." Cameron's voice is pleading and it burrows down into my soul. My heart is so fucking heavy and my head follows suit, but nevertheless I nod. I know what he did, but that won't stop the fact that Simon will never leave me alone until he's gotten what he wants. And Cameron is probably the only one who could ever stop him. Cam sets me back up in the chair, my eyes constantly going to his shoulder where the blood seems to have stopped. I cannot believe that I fucking stabbed him.

I sit in the chair as he wraps the ropes around my wrists once again, also handing me my now cleaned pocketknife. Cameron takes root in the back corner behind some boxes, knowing that Simon will be back soon. Cameron pulls out his phone, his brows furrow but he looks back at me. "Zack says he's on his way, baby girl. This is all gonna be over soon."

I don't reply, but the door opens and Simon's face flies to mine, and the tremors return to my body. I close my eyes, not wanting to look at him.

"What a good girl, waiting for me like I told you to." His voice is laden with malice as he walks in towards me.

Suddenly, flashes of the night my parents were murdered cloud my mind. All of my life, I've lived with this fog surrounding the event but in this moment, there are sparks of pure clarity. I can see the wood grain floor speckled with blood. The empty stare in my mother's eyes as she lay on her bed, already growing cold. A boy, only a couple years older than me, staring me down as I hid in the depth of my closet and praying he doesn't *really* see me.

Cameron. That blonde boy with the big green eyes...

It was Cameron and a man who I can only assume was his dad. Images keep flickering through my mind, a man with a gruff face and dark eyes yelling at little Cameron. The sound of my own father, who had never been a man who took shit from anyone or feared anything, begging for his life. *Begging for his life— and it thrills something inside me. My heart is pounding; hoping, waiting, praying for it to happen.*

But then the boy and his dad are out in the hallway, and I can't let this moment pass. If they leave me with my dad and without my mom, nothing good is going to happen to me. Something *very, very* bad will happen. Daddy will blame me somehow, someway. He always does.

My memory jumps then to me standing over my father as he was tied up on his bed and a bloodied knife in my hand.

It was me. I killed my father—not Cameron, *me.* I had been desperate for that night to be the end of him so that I could stop living every day in fear.

I let out a soft gasp as the memory slams into me. I can't let Cameron take Simon out, I can't let him take the blame for something that I know that should be mine to claim. *Not again.* It's the least I can do. A sense of resolve settles over me as I look towards Simon, a confident and assured grin settles over me.

Moments pass in what feels like slow motion, a realization dawns on me and I now know what I have to do, Cameron can't be the one to kill him.

It has to be me.

As soon as Simon is close enough to me, I see Cameron stand, and I know that this is my moment.

"Mine," I say out loud with this unknown confidence, as Simon's face contorts with shock as I lift the knife. There's a split second of consternation on his face before I again experience the familiar sensation of a blade in my hand cutting through flesh. It's only a matter of seconds between when I claimed the kill for myself, and his throat being slit before me.

His hands immediately raises to the slice as he tries to speak, but blood gurgles out of his mouth. He falls to his knees then crumples to the floor, blood pooling around him. Cameron is instantly at my side as I drop the knife and almost immediately lose consciousness, my body falling to the ground. What have I done?

Simon Maher is dead.

25
COLD SHOWER
LEYLA

The world around me is blank.

I feel the ground beneath me moving, but I can't seem to open my eyes. Am I dead? Is this Hell? I don't know what happened, but I sense the world moving faster around me. I open my eyes and everything blurs together before slowly snapping into focus. Turning my head, I see a worried Cameron in the driver's seat.

Car. I'm in a car, and we're going... somewhere. His knuckles grip the steering wheel, white from tension; and he looks like he's been crying. A quiet groan escapes me when I start to sit up but my head is killing me. His head whips towards me, his face instantly softening.

"Hey hey, Cherry-girl. Take it easy, slow movements." His voice is so sweet and gentle that I feel my breath catch. My eyes focus and the events of the day pass through me in a whirlwind.

The meeting with Alex. The phone call with Cameron.

Simon. *Simon… I killed Simon.* It sounds so absurd to even think to myself, but I know it's true. I can feel the pocketknife clutched in my hand, and I can see the blood *spouting* from his neck.

I begin to hyperventilate, but his hand is on my cheek, trying to calm me down with a gentle caress with the pad of his thumb. "Baby girl, you're safe. We're almost home and we're gonna get you cleaned up. I promised you there was nowhere you could go that would keep me from you and I meant it. This is gonna be just fine. You're gonna be okay. I won't stop fixing it until you are."

———

I don't remember closing my eyes, but the next time they're open, we're parked and I'm in his arms as carries me into his house. I lean my head against his chest and his touch is gentle, yet purposeful. I have so much I want to say, it's like there's a block that just won't let me do anything about it. He's here. I'm safe. Simon is dead.

Once inside, he gently sets me onto his bed. The world around me is coming in and out of focus, but the constant is that he's here. *My* Cameron is here.

"Cherry, I'm gonna start the shower, okay? I'll just be in that room right there, you can see me from here." His voice is so gentle, somehow once again knowing exactly what I needed to hear. He takes the time to explain everything to me that he does. I force myself to give a soft nod, a shiver running down my spine. Moments pass before I hear running water and just like he promised, he's back in front of me. Cameron kneels down in front of me, gently lifting my chin, thoroughly examining me for injuries.

"C'mon, baby girl, I'm gonna undress you now, okay? Let me take care of you," he adds on. My face must be expressing some sort of fear, but he doesn't relent. "I've got you, Cherry. You're safe." He repeats as he begins to peel off my blood-soaked clothes.

Simon is dead and I was the one who killed him.

Cameron takes his time undressing me until I'm fully naked. He stands up carefully, holding his arm out for me. I slowly reach my hands out as he leads me to the bathroom with the shower running. He steps into the shower first, fully clothed, but it doesn't seem to bother him. He pulls me into the shower with him, my body tensing up from the shock of water hitting my clammy skin.

"That's my good girl. Just breathe, okay?" Cameron's voice is so relaxing and calm. Pulling out a rag, he lathers up the soap and begins his gentle ministrations along my arms. I feel my legs giving out, and, as if he and I are one, he helps me to the ground and gently speaks into my hair. "You're safe, you're clean, and you're going to be okay."

I believe him, too. Without hesitation, thought, or reason. I don't know why, but I just *do.*

We sit in the shower for what seems like hours as he gently lathers shampoo into my hair and begins to comb his fingers through it, unraveling any knots with the care that you'd expect a giant taking care of a sick kitten. Maybe that's apt. Maybe I'm losing my mind, after all.

No. Be in the moment. Nothing good will come from questioning anything today, there's no telling where my mind will take me but I know that if it's not pertaining to this exact moment, I don't want to go.

A soft breath escapes my lips as he massages my scalp. The things that I know, and the things that I feel, are at war with each other, but at this moment I know it's where I'm meant to be.

I close my eyes and take a deep breath as Cameron wraps his arms around me. *I am in love with this man; there's no way that I can be. I shouldn't be.*

"We can talk about that later, Cherry. Let me just take care of you right now." My cheeks flush with embarrassment. Shit, I said all that out loud, didn't I? Cameron doesn't pause what he is doing, worry etching his features.

Cameron slowly stands, my body already missing the warmth of his touch. Turning off the water, he gently steps out of the shower and grabs a towel before turning towards me. He cautiously picks me up, helping me stand as I step out of the shower close to him.

Simon Maher is dead.

Words are still too hard and my entire body aches. As I look up at him, his face is lined with pain and concern as he wraps me up in the towel. Slowly patting me dry, he wraps me up again, picking me up in his strong, steady arms and carries me to his bed.

My body is still as I watch him go to his dresser and pull out a pair of gray sweats and an old Red Wings t-shirt. He stands in front of me, his clothes still drenched, and helps me get dressed.

As if I weigh nothing, he picks me up again, and lays me down onto his cool pillow, pulling the comforter up over me. Leaning down, Cameron places a kiss on my forehead.

"Sleep Cherry, I will be right here when you wake up." My body sags into the comfort of his bed, as I fall into a dreamless sleep.

26

WORRY LINES

CAMERON

Standing in my room as I watch her sleep, my clothes are still sticking limp and heavy against my skin, but I don't care. I can't relax until I know she's deep into her sleep. Leyla's face is full of worry lines, her brow creases as she hugs my pillow tight. A shiver hits my body, and I crack my neck. Once I've convinced my brain that she's okay, I finally give myself permission to get changed and stitch up my damn shoulder.

It has to be the adrenaline wearing off as the feeling burning in my shoulder crawls down my arm like liquid fire. It's uncomfortable, but at least I've been able to stave off this feeling until Leyla was asleep. Glancing back to her from the bathroom, I feel this sick sense of calm settle over me. She said she's in love with me, that she shouldn't be, but she does anyway.

I shake my head to focus back on what was going on with

my body. I open the wooden doors underneath my sink, grab my medical kit, and immediately begin cleaning up my wound.

Fuck. Fuck. FUCK.

The pain radiates down my arm and I realize how much this fucking sucks. I pull up the sleeve that is now caked onto my arm with dried— and some spots, still sticky— blood. There's nothing I can do but wince as the shirt pulls some of the dried bloodied bits away, not wanting to make a noise and risk waking Leyla. Blood slowly drips down my arm, but I grit my teeth, ripping open the sanitizing pads and manage to make my curses just grunts as the alcohol hits the open gash.

"Damn, Cherry, you got me good," I hiss through my teeth. Closing my eyes, I focus on the next part, which is always my least favorite part. I thread the needle and wince as I pinch together the open wound. The needle pokes through my skin. It's no more than an inch and a half long so it won't take many stitches. Focusing on my breathing, I continue methodically until it's closed. Cleaning up the area around it once more, I place the gauze bandage on and tape it up. I take another deep breath as I look in the mirror, realizing that I look like utter shit.

Turning on the faucet, I splash some cold water on my face, hoping that I'm able to clean myself up completely. I turn to look at Leyla who is still sound asleep in my bed. My bed, where my girl belongs. I don't want to wake her, but now there's the task at hand of cleaning up the warehouse where Simon's body lies now, untouched. Pulling out my phone, I sigh as I text Zack.

Cameron: Hey, need a cleanup. Got a guy?

Normally it's me. I'm one who is meticulous and thorough to my standards, but this wasn't done in the safety of my confines. This was messy and done by someone who hasn't killed before— well, and had to deal with the consequences. Like remembering. And cleaning up blood. Damn it, what the hell am I going to do about all *that?*

I put my phone down. As I sit down on the bed next to Leyla, I run my hands through her hair and smile softly. I feel the soft buzz of my phone.

> Zackasaurus Rex: What kind of clean-up?

> Cameron: Deep cleaning. Got a little carried away

> Zackasaurus Rex: They'll take care of it. Do you need an alibi?

> Cameron: Can you scrub the cameras and put us at home, location-wise?

> Zackasarus Rex: Insulted you think I haven't already done that. Consider everything covered. Take care of her. Talk soon

Knowing that Zack has this part covered, I feel my shoulders relax for the first time all day, and my head falls into my hands. I let myself go into that place that I try so hard to avoid going into. I'm not that person anymore, I only take those out of play that truly deserve it.

An idea blooms to life in my head and I can't help but let a curve form on my lips. Maybe once Leyla realizes what she did was okay, I could show her the way, show her truly what good she could do for this world. We could do that all together.

I'm quickly thrown from my obsessive thoughts as I hear a soft whimper coming from Leyla, and I'm there in a heartbeat. I'm there because my girl will never have to suffer alone again — that is if she trusts me. I will make her trust me again, because she loves me, she said so herself.

My thoughts stop as she whimpers again. My tone is hushed, "Cherry, it's just a dream. It's only a dream, it's not real. You're safe, you're home with me." I run my hand through her silken hair, my hand a constant comfort for her so long as she wants it.

Suddenly, Leyla's eyes fly open and she shoots up into a sitting position. She begins looking around frantically. I give her space but gently place a hand on her arm to calm her.

"Hey, Cherry-girl, you're safe. You're at my house." Her dual-toned eyes stare off into the distance for a moment, until she comes back and focuses on me. "There's my good girl." I smile sweetly, I gently place my other hand under her chin to lift up her head.

"Are you back with me now?" I ask gently enough that I don't startle her and send her into another spiral. Her lips purse but she nods.

"Yea, I'm here."

I have never realized how fragile Leyla Clarkson truly is and has been, until just now. Seeing her look like she was afraid of her own shadow shatters me, but I know that she will ever be alone again. I'm going to teach my girl to protect herself, and maybe even find a sense of self again.

I love this woman. There isn't anything in this world more perfect and flawless than her.

"You wanna get something to eat? You could use some food," I say as I gently stand up off the edge of the bed and walk around to her side of it, offering her my hand. It's probably 5:30 in the morning by this point and she hadn't eaten anything since yesterday.

"Yea, food sounds good. Then you can... can... start telling me what the fuck just happened." Her voice is sounding a little more confident than what it had been like for the hours prior.

"I'm just glad you're okay, princess. I thought I lost you for a minute there." My smile is plastered wide on my face. The true joy of knowing that she's mine again and that I didn't ruin anything is starting to simmer just below my skin.

"You did and you have a lot of explaining to do," her voice is harder than I've ever heard it before. That smile that was there just a moment ago, falls into a face of emotionlessness. I'm not in the clear. There is a fuck ton of work that has to be done and I may have just dug my own grave or severed any chance of redemption of us ever being happy together. I will make this right. I have to.

27
ANSWER ME
LEYLA

Memories slam into me like a tidal wave and I don't know that I'm ready to handle them. Not yet.

Cameron was there the day my parents were killed. I had just killed someone too. This wasn't the first time that I had killed either.

Can I really hold anything against Cameron when I've become just as bad as him?

I sit on the edge of his bed, eyes tracing the bare skin of his chest. A scar stretches across it, something I hadn't noticed before. It catches the morning sunlight pouring through the window as he moves around the kitchen.

Guilt stabs me like a blade when I see the bandage on his shoulder to cover a wound. The one I put there— I really stabbed him. I did that. I fucking stabbed him.

God, how do I move on from that? Can I ever get past it—

especially knowing he's the one who killed my parents? Was it just him? Or someone else too? My head's swimming with questions, and I don't even know where to start.

"Cherry?"

I jump at the sudden voice. My heart slams against my ribs as I turn toward him standing in the doorway. "Hmm?" I murmur, trying to push down the chaos in my mind. My expression slips into something softer— fake, but softer. And damn it, there go those butterflies again, fluttering in my stomach like they have no business doing. I shrink inward as he crosses the space between us.

"Breakfast is ready. I know it's probably the last thing on your mind, but you've gotta eat something."

His voice is so gentle, it physically hurts. I need his touch. I need *him*— but my heart and my head are at war. I just nod, unsure, as he offers me his hand.

I want to turn away. I should walk out that door and never look back. That would be the smart move; the safe one.

But I take his hand anyway.

His fingers curl around mine in a soft squeeze, and I feel the guilt pouring off of him like a second skin. I see the pain in his face, and it hurts. My internal war rages over the choices that I want to just have the answers to and show that I know what to do, but I bury it, letting him lead me forward.

I'll get my answers. I'm better than this.

We walk to his little kitchen table and he pulls out the chair for me as I sit down. He walks to the counter grabbing the two plates that he prepared and places one in front of me. Our eyes connect and a sad smile sits on Cameron's face, but we don't say a word. We don't do anything but start eating.

The silence crushes us, broken only by the clinking of utensils against plates. I bite into the pancakes and a small moan escapes before I can stop it. My cheeks flush as I glance up. He's grinning now, like really grinning. I sigh and give in to his perfect face.

I'll talk, but I'm going to talk about what matters. I'm not going to play like everything is alright when *I just fucking killed someone.*

"I have a lot of questions, Cam. And I'm really confused. And... honestly, I don't even know where to start." I relent and finally break the silence that has crept over the atmosphere. Cameron opens his mouth, my hand flies up stopping him. "No, it's my turn to speak, I will tell you when it's your turn to answer."

He nods and my stomach is in knots. "Why— no how did–" the questions I've got spiraling around in my head don't slow, I close my eyes trying to keep my mind calm.

"Sorry. I just... I guess my first question is, are you okay? I didn't mean to stab you." I keep my voice steady, even though my face betrays the guilt clawing at me. "I'm sorry. Really."

I gently trace the edge of the bandage over his bicep and flinch in empathetic pain. Cameron gives me a small smile, and nods. "I'm okay, Leyla, I'm okay. I stitched myself up and I'll be good as new. You didn't do it on purpose." His voice doesn't waver, but he looks at me knowingly. "Ask me the real question," he says. "The one that got interrupted yesterday."

Fuck, was that only yesterday?— No, fucking focus Leyla.

"I already know you were there the day my parents died. I don't need to know the whole story just yet, but– I need to know why."

Flashes of memory keep hitting me since the kidnapping, but they're still fragmented. I feel seasick, too much information and feelings trying to settle into my brain all at once. Some bits feel a little familiar, and I recall the moments of clarity I had the day before. But the smell of blood, the fear, the pounding of my head are skewing my recent memories. I find myself holding to the edge of the table, as though I really am at sea.

Before yesterday, I had never felt strong— and I might not feel it now, but damn it, I'm going to try.

"It wasn't just you— it was your dad too, wasn't it?" My voice is quiet but clear. I don't bother explaining what I mean, I know he knows. "And you saw me that day? Why didn't you kill me too?" A million questions sit at the tip of my tongue, but I let them sit on the backburner.

How do I ask him if I was the one who killed my dad?

"How much do you remember, Cherry?" His face serious but contemplative.

"I-I didn't remember anything from before my parents were killed until yesterday when I– when I killed Simon." The words are bitter off my tongue, words catching in my throat as I don't break eye contact with him. "I-I remember my dad– he would take me to this clearing in the woods, where there were cairns or maybe they were tombstones?"

Cameron's face doesn't falter, as if he's not phased by what I'm saying. "He would take me to the garage all the time and I would watch as he would... have people tied up in there. Dad always said he was showing people the right way. I was so young, I didn't know any better. Oh god, I watched him– h-he was a rapist, wasn't he? He was, and that's why you... your dad killed him?"

He's holding my gaze with the firmness his arms had when carrying me through the door last night. I should feel safe, it's Cam and he's telling me the truth, *my* truth— but I've never been more terrified in my life. The truth is going to fuck me up more than the last couple of days have on their own. Yet, I have to know. There's no moving forward without the truth.

"Leyla, your dad was a serial rapist, yes; and he killed his victims. Your mom helped him with hiding the bodies, they had a whole system, and they used you as bait." Cameron's words hit me like bricks as the air rushes out from my lungs. "My dad is– was a killer back then. He was known as The Whispering Killer. Your parents were my first time going out with him. He trained me my entire life to follow in his footsteps."

He rubs his hands together as his gaze falters and stares down. I'm holding my breath with anticipation as he takes a deep breath himself, looks up, and continues.

"The people we killed were bad people, that's why he didn't kill you that day. When we found out you were in the house still, he made it his personal mission to keep you safe. To keep you out of harm's way. Then when my dad started getting sick, he would forget things, he got mean— violent and started taking things out on my mom and I—"

Cameron's eyes brimmed with tears and, even though it felt like the world was falling apart, I was up and I pulled him up with me, wrapping my arms around him to comfort him. Cameron's face is full of impassive emotions that I can tell he's trying to keep to himself, but the pain in his eyes is telling me an entire story, that isn't the one he's telling me right now.

"He walked out of the room after killing your mom, he was preparing me to kill your dad. I was going to do it too, I was so fucking afraid that if I didn't he would hurt me again..." his voice is watery as he closes his eyes taking a deep breath again. "I walked into your parent's room, and you were standing over him, with one of my dad's scalpels, and your dad was already dead. I moved so fucking fast getting you out of there because I knew what he would do to you if he saw you there, and I couldn't let that fucking happen."

His large arms wrapped around me and kissed the crown of my head. "Because of what you did that day, he laid off of me for months, he didn't touch me– didn't hurt me for months after that and I never knew how to thank you for that. I was, and still am, in your debt for that day."

I place a gentle kiss on his cheek, his is voice still hushed, his eyes distant like he's not really here with me. "My dad killed my mom one year after your parents' deaths. I swore that day I would continue on taking out the horrible people in the world, to prevent people like my father from ever walking this earth again. So that no one would ever go through that pain again."

My arms wrap around him. I just want to surround him with the feeling that he isn't really alone.

Cameron takes a deep breath, a small spark of life breathe

into his cold eyes, almost fully back to me now, just more than there was a moment ago. "My dad was a terrible person. My dad hurt me, and made me feel worthless every fucking day of my life. Michael Curtis, made my life a living hell, while still giving me a childhood full of lessons that I don't think I could explain. I felt indebted to a man, who I truly didn't owe a single thing to. I was... I *am* a part of the monster, that deserves redemption and the chance to truly make this world better."

I should hate him. I should be horrified by what he's done, and what part he played in my life. I don't, though. Some fucked up part of me loves him even more.

"No more secrets?" My voice whispers, as I wipe a tear that falls down his cheek. I see the uncertainty of what he's admitted spiraling around him. The fear that I'm going to run.

I'm not.

"No more secrets. I don't deserve you, Cherry, but I'm keeping you. You're mine."

My eyes connect with his, and I feel my chest tightening from the unforeseen whirlwind of stress, unending questions, and just utter shame and disappointment that I'm currently feeling. I have so many damn questions, and I want to know everything about them.

"Tell me about my parents? Because the people you say they are, and the people I remember... aren't really making sense for me and I just don't know what to believe right now." I catch every movement of Cameron's face as his brows shoot up the way he looks at me sends a rush down my spine, I shiver and shake my head. "Please, Cammy? I don't think you understand, I don't know much from my childhood."

Cameron's brows are knitted in this constant furrow, I can practically see the gears turning inside his head trying to begin how to explain it all. His blonde hair falling down in front of his face, I gently brush his hair back, the tension radiating off of him.

"How much do you know?" His voice doesn't even sound like him, the black of his pupils push out the green of his eyes. I watch Cameron descend into this place that I can tell he doesn't go into often. His shoulders curl in slightly, his dark eyes now connected with mine in an unbreaking stare.

"I remember the cemetery, I remember..." I bite my lower lip in an attempt to remember anything from back then, other than what I've already said. "Nothing."

The disappointment in my voice is palpable, I've never been able to have that singular breakthrough moment that all those characters in the books and movies do. Therapists, treatments, none of it ever were able to break through that mental wall that was put up for me. It's why I need him, and I need him to tell me.

"Your parents killed eight people— three men and five women. Mainly your father, but they would take you out to public places and have you wander around. Knowing the person they were targeting would stop and help you. They would take them to your garage–"

I interrupt Cameron with a soft gasp, as this flash of my dad walking a blonde-haired woman into our backyard garage. I shake my head trying to clear that plaque that keeps growing in my mind.

"I–I... No, Cameron..." My heart is telling me that this can't be true, that my own father wouldn't have done something like this.

"Leyla..." his voice deceptively calm, he gently reaches up, rubbing his knuckle along my cheek. I should pull away, I shouldn't let this happen to me, not again. And yet, going against all my instincts I gently lean into his touch.

"I don't know if I'm actually ready to hear all of this, Cam," My voice comes out of me barely above a whisper. I can't even begin to imagine what's actually happening. I know that above all else, Cameron wouldn't lie to me. Not after all of this. Cameron slowly walks away from me towards a backpack that was sitting in the corner of his room; somehow, I hadn't noticed it. I watch as he rummages around in the bag, turning around he gently places a manilla folder on the table next to me.

"This is everything, I had, my father had, and the police had on your parents, okay? I know my dad did some... some pretty horrific things, but he worked on a system. He took out those that were the darkest of the dark. He killed people who killed others, who hurt others, and those who preyed on innocent people. Your parents took advantage of you— they played it off as if they were taking you to the fair, or the park or mall. They manipulated you into thinking that there was no other way, it was their own personal gain, and you were literally an unknowing pawn."

He continues after a brief pause, "The day your parents died, I made it my own personal goal to never let anything bad happen to you ever again. But I failed you with Simon." Another silence, this time anger flashes on his face before being extinguished by force.

"All my protections I had in place to protect you, but I let him slip through the cracks..." He shakes his head. "I need you to know it's just us now. No one will ever take you for granted or take advantage of you ever again. You are mine. Forever." He plants a kiss on my cheek, his hand cupping the back of my head as he pulls me closer to him.

His possessive tone sends a shiver down my body and I'm sure there's something wrong with me, as a need floods my system.

I think I've short-circuited.

"I want to help you." The words leave my mouth before I truly process what I'm saying. "Knowing that someone like Simon– like my parents, that there is no longer any way they are going to hurt anyone else ever again? I want you to teach me. Help me be like you. Help me fix the mistakes."

If you can't beat them, kill them.

I admire so much what Cameron has done— and what he's done for me. Yeah, it's fucked up, but justice is never so black and white. And if I can save anyone from this fucked up reality that I find myself in, I want to do it.

I've never really felt a strong sense of direction in my life; even school has just been something to do. But this... It feels right. The words play over and over in my head, and I'm more certain with each repetition.

A moment of charged silence sits between us, our bodies still pressed against each other. Safe– despite everything that's happened, the safest I've ever felt is in his arms. Right here, right now.

"Fuck, Cherry, I'm pretty sure that's the hottest thing I've ever heard." His arms tighten around me, and his eyes darken as he smirks. Cameron's hands tilt my chin, our eyes forced to connect. Wordlessly, he knows what I need and our lips crash in a cacophony of emotions.

Cameron Curtis is going to be my undoing, and I don't want it any other fucking way.

28
INTERTWINED
CAMERON

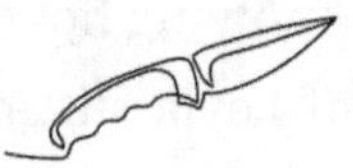

oly shit I am so fucking in love with this woman. I run my hands through her hair as I walk her back into the counter. Her body is so fucking responsive to my touch, it sends a thrill through me.

I don't want this to stop.

"Cherry," my voice is breathless as I kiss along her jawline. Her sighs filling the room, her breath hitches. My cock struggles against the seam of my gray sweats as I bite at her neck, feeling as her body arches, and she moans. The sounds she makes is the most fucking beautiful music to my ears. I can't fucking stand how perfect Leyla is. Her curves press up against me and it's as if we were made to never be apart. I have all of her and she has all of me too.

"Tell me, Cherry," I begin. The voice that comes out of me is low and practically a growl. Her head falls back and her eyes roll to the back of her head as my hands run down her stomach and into the waistband of her pants. I run the pads of my fingers over her slick pussy and let out a pained groan.

"You're so fucking wet for me, Cherry, tell me how much you want me." I slip a single finger into her slick cunt, Leyla's back arches as she lets a squeak out.

"I need you Cameron—I—oh *fuck*..." I add another finger. A full body shiver racks her body and she pants, her eyes heavy and hooded. I smirk just knowing how fucking reactive she is to my touch. The thought of Leyla slitting Simon's throat rushes through me and my breath hitches with the thought of the things that she could do to me sends a whole body rush that I never felt before.

I pull her close to me, my fingers crook inside her and she moans. "You're fucking hypnotic, Cherry..." I feel her walls clenching around my fingers, I pull out of her pussy and she lets out a sweet little whimper. The ways that I know that she's wholly mine with the noises she makes.

"C-Cameron..." Leyla's breathy voice is desperate and I love it. This fucking perfect woman is mine, and I'm free to do what I want with her. I wrap my hands around her legs and lift her up.

"Where do you want me to take you, Cherry? 'Cause I can do it right here, or I can do it in the bed. It doesn't matter where because you belong to me now, and I intend to teach you every way to Sunday all the ways that you're my good girl." Her legs tighten around my hips as my hands sit comfortably on her waist.

Her hands run through my hair as she leans in and kisses my jaw, her teeth gently grazing my skin as my hands instinctively grip her waist tighter. "You're driving me crazy, Cherry girl." I playfully nip at her ear and she giggles.

"Take me Cameron, right here, right now. I can't hold out any more…" The red crawls up from her chest and neck, taking claim on her face as she traces my chest.

Placing her on the counter, I shimmy off her pants that are so rudely in my way. My cock is throbbing against my sweats that still hasn't been given the release it so badly needs, it begins to hurt.

"Spread those pretty thighs for me. I'm quite hungry, you see, and your sweet, sweet pussy is what I'm craving." I press her legs even further apart than she does and my tongue lathes along the length of her pussy, circling around the sensitive bundle of nerves that sends her back arching.

Her hands play with her tits, giving attention to her nipples, and she lets out the most beautiful moan to ever grace my ears.

"You're so fucking wet, Cherry. All of this is for me?" I know that all this foreplay is driving her wild, proven by her hips bucking forwards as I place a kiss on her clit.

I pull her down off the counter, wordlessly flipping her around and bending her over the counter. I drop my pants freeing my pleading cock, it sits against my chest as I spread her open for me and line myself up with her entrance. I thrust my cock into her dripping pussy without warning; Leyla lets out a moan that sends a shiver through me.

"Mine." I growl as I thrust into her, her walls clenching around my cock.

"Cameron–I– Oh god, Cammy—" Leyla pants in time to the bruising pace of my cock. I wrap her hair around my fist and pull her back into my body and she lets out another moan. "Cam–Cam–I'm gonna..I'm gonna." My balls tighten with the impending release knowing that I'm barreling towards with her.

"No, you be a good girl, not yet. I didn't say you could come yet." Leyla lets out a whimper as she clenches around my cock, she pants as my thrust slows to an almost painful pace. Pulling her head back by her hair, she looks at me with tears pricking her eyes, a devilish grin on my face. "*Beg*, baby girl."

"Cameron–please–*please*—" sweat drips down her back from the relentless punishment her pussy is receiving. I pull my cock out to the tip, and she whimpers as I flip her around so that my beautiful girl faces me.

"I want to see you come, baby girl. You belong to me now, and you come when I tell you to. Understand?" Without giving her a moment to respond I slam myself to the hilt inside her and she screams as her back arches.

"Cameron!"

My name is like a prayer on her lips, pleasure coursing through me at the mere sound. I resume my bruising pace, my own release building up. I lean over her, my hands resting above her head on the counter. I bite her nipples in slow but rough pulls, and she lets out a scream that makes the world stop as both of our orgasms hit the peak.

"Fall for me baby girl, let go."

Her body shakes as my own climax hits me filling her sweet pussy with both of our releases. I stand over her as her body shivers slowly subside. Leyla pants as her shaking arms fail to hold up her own bodyweight.

"I've got you, Cherry." I wrap my arms around her and pick her up, carrying her to the bathroom to shower her off once more. She wraps her arms around me kissing my shoulder, a whimper as I place her down, but don't let go.

"Can you stand?"

She tries to hide the smile on her face. "What, like you have some magic dick or something?" Leyla teases, and I pinch her ass. Leyla yelps as she playfully tries to push off of me. "Cam!" Her joy is palpable, it flutters around the room, I grab her chin forcing her to look at me.

"I would say that orgasm speaks for itself," the woman of my dreams laughs. I lean over and start the shower, my cock clearly already ready for round two.

Leyla steps into the stream of the water, it drips off her body and I can't help but admire every single part of her. I step into the shower with her and the water is warm and consumes the both of us. "Have I told you how fucking beautiful you are, Cherry?" I see the little kernel of self-doubt settle in on Leyla's face, I never want that to be there again. I want her to know every single day how perfect she truly is.

"Hey, listen to me." I press her into the wall, getting onto my knees in front of her and kiss her calves. "These–" I move up to her thighs, kissing each of the little scars that litter them, making sure she knows she will never hurt again. "Mine." I kiss each hip, her stomach, each breast. "Mine." The water pounds over the two of us, but her piercing eyes never leave mine. Moving over to her front shoulders, then down her arms, I grab her wrists and kiss them, a gentle press of my lips to her palms, then each individual finger. "All mine, Cherry."

Pulling myself into a standing position, I gently place my hands on her cheeks. "These? Also mine." I kiss her lips, her nose, her cheeks. Her eyes fluttering close, I kiss each eye, then place a kiss on her forehead. "I have known since we were kids that you are mine, Leyla. You have consumed my every waking thought, and I will stop at nothing to make sure you know how fucking loved you are." Tears mix with the water streaming down my girls face, and I kiss them away.

"I love you Leyla, I love you so much."

She keeps her eyes closed as she nods, no more words pass between us as I clean her up with gentle caresses and my sandalwood bodywash. "I love you, too." She whispers, just barely above the sound of the shower.

"That's my good girl." I flip her around again, and grin devilishly. "Ready for round two?"

Leyla lets out a yelp and her eyes darken, "Here?!"

"Leyla, I plan on taking you in every single place we can in this home." She lets out a gasp, and smirks.

"Oh," Leyla bites her lip and grins, sinking down to her knees as she wastes no time putting her beautiful lips around my cock. Her tongue lathes around my shaft and my hips buck instinctively. How does she *DO that?* I hear her gag, I go to pull out but she pushes herself further onto my cock, she looks up at me through her thick lashes. Her teeth gently graze my cock, sending a rush of pleasure and pain screaming through my body.

"Fuck– Ley–" My head falls back as I feel my own orgasm building up in my balls, they tighten. She does that thing again with her fucking tongue and I'm a goner. My cum shoots down the back of her throat in streams and she takes it all. She pulls off my cock with a pop, wiping the side of her mouth off. I stand there panting for a moment, stars dancing in my field of vision, truly trying to figure out how the fuck this magic woman just did that.

"In case you weren't aware—you're also mine now Cam." Her seductive tone sends a shiver through my body, and holy fuck are we going to have fun.

29
TAKE CARE OF YOU
LEYLA

I never pictured my life would be this.

I never imagined that I would be this fucking lucky. You would think being told that the man you are dating was one of the reasons your parents were dead wouldn't be a reason to leave someone. Somehow it isn't an issue.

Besides, it wasn't him— it was his father; and I remember better than anyone what it's like to live in the shadow of people who only took advantage of you. Their death had taken away so much from me. In its stead, however, it's now given me a whole new outlook on life and I honestly could not be happier than where I'm at.

I look at Cameron sleeping next to me in his bed, the warmth emanating off his body covers me and it's a feeling that I never want to stop. What we did last night was a level of trust and joining that doesn't just happen to anyone, it was a breaking point for us and there's no going back now. I don't truly know if it could ever be replicated.

Instinctively, I inch closer to his chiseled chest, my body melting into his as if we were made to be one. He is home. My home. His chest rises and falls in even breaths and I stare at it, his perfectly defined chest is littered with scars from a past no one was there to protect him from, and the cuts from what we did last night. Camerons arms tighten around me like a vice, pulling me closer than should be possible. A soft chuckle shakes his chest as he gently kisses the crown of my head.

"Morning, Cherry." Cameron's voice is low, silken like velvet. I didn't think it was possible, but this man's morning voice is by far the hottest thing I've ever experienced. Gently, I try to pull away from his bear-like grasp to no avail as he gives me a squeeze keeping me close to his body. "Let's just stay here for a little while. Just us."

I nod as he loosens his grip on me, still not letting me go. There's this little part of me that is screaming at me that somehow, I don't deserve this. "Yea, just us— only us." Everything that's happened doesn't even feel real at this moment nor do I really care that it's happened. It all comes rushing over me, I know for certain that no matter what happens, I am in love with Cameron Curtis, I don't care what he's done, then or now, I know the real man behind the curtain. He's not perfect or a carbon copy of every other man on this earth, but he doesn't have to be.

"Cam? Can I ask you something?" My voice quivers slightly, but I don't let it show on my face. His deep green eyes narrow in on me and he gently brushes a stray hair off my face.

"Anything, Cherry, I will answer anything you need to know." His hand subconsciously traces along the silky material of my nightgown.

A shaky exhale as I close my eyes, open them and look at the man in front of me. "Teach me?" Cameron's hand stills, his breath catching.

"Teach you what?" Hesitation prickles his response.

"Teach me how to never be defenseless again? Teach me how to make sure people like Simon never get that power over me?" The things that I felt when Simon had taken me, the way that I was helpless to his advances. I didn't stand a chance, and this entire time, he was the one who had been tormenting my psyche, breaking it apart bit by bit.

I won't let that happen to me again.

"I want to help you. You know, do what you do. I want to make this world a better place so that monsters like Simon don't ever get the chance to do that to someone else."

Cameron is quiet for a moment, I could see the gears turning in his head. I want control in my life, something that up until last night I didn't think was anything I would ever achieve. Being here, with Cameron, I'm in control again. Well, at least I'm beginning to be.

Cameron's face looks torn, and I know what I'm asking of him isn't something... *normal.* I'm not asking him to teach me how to drive stick or how to properly swing a golf club— I'm asking him to teach me how to kill with purpose and control. It's not something that anyone should ever ask for, yet here I am.

My heart begins to race, the silence that ensued is deafening, my nerves reaching a level that was almost painful. Gently pulling away, I look at him. "Cam?"

"Leyla, I need you to know what you're asking of me," Cameron's voice is one level and has an eerie calm to it that has the hairs on my arm standing on edge. A chill runs through my body, but I nod.

"I know what I'm asking you, Cameron." My voice, confident as it may be, doesn't give room for any further discussion. I need to be stronger. I need to not be afraid.

There's another beat of silence before he answers. "Okay. I'll teach you everything I know." A smile grows on my face, and he mirrors it in return. His dimple makes an appearance as he raises a hand, gently cupping my cheek. "You don't have much to learn on how to be strong. You're already the strongest person I've ever met." The conviction and truth in his words settle over me like a blanket on a cold winter's day. It's then when it hits me and the words tumble out before I could even try to stop them.

"I love you."

Cameron stills and he smiles, the dimple that made an appearance creases even deeper in, his eyes crinkle at the corners.

"Lucky for you, Cherry, I love you too."

That right there is how I know, this man is to be the death of me, and I'd be ready with open arms. I am unequivocally and totally in love, and he loved me right back; something that I had only ever dreamt of but now was finally mine.

Cameron gently kisses the top of my head, and I know that my life is forever changed. Nothing will be the same ever again.

Cameron must pick up on the change in my mood, his arms wrapping around me and the warmth that envelops me, centers me back into the moment.

His voice is quiet, his emerald eyes forcing me to keep focus as he speaks, "You okay, Cherry?"

A whirlwind of emotions settles in my chest and I don't even know where to begin. The weight of everything that's happened this week comes rushing through me and I let out a huge exhale.

"I'm okay... I just never thought that I'd both gain and lose everything all over again. I never thought I'd get all the answers to what happened." I clear my throat knowing that no matter what comes out of my mouth, Cameron will have an answer for me.

"Can I ask you something now?" Cameron's voice betrays the calm demeanor present on his face. I nod with a soft smile and my back straightens.

"Anything, baby. You've been honest with me, I promise you anything you want to know, I'll give you the honesty you've given me."

Cameron's face regards me with such patience and kindness. I never really felt that I deserved this amount of respect from anyone, but somehow Cameron is proving to me that I'm worthy. Maybe we can actually be... *something.*

"That's okay, I know that was a big ask of me. I just want to know where we stand when I start our lessons." Cameron bites his cheek, a habit I've noticed he does when he's overthinking things.

"When do we start? I wanna see where you do it all, cause I

know everything there is about The Whispering Killer's motives, I know you kill at a different location and then place them in a new location. I know it's usually only people who have been suspected or are killers themselves. Do you ever regret killing those people?" The questions come pouring out of me unrelenting and without pause.

I look up to him, a smile grows on his face, he's fucking enjoying this and I can't help but match the smile. "What?" My face scrunches teasingly as he leans in and kisses me.

"You just never cease to amaze me." His words are gentle, but hit my soul in a way that makes me feel like this is the safest place in the world.

"You're evading the questions." Leaning in, I kiss him in return, fully knowing the game that he's playing with me.

"Not evading, just trying to figure out how to answer them for you." Cameron laughs softly, "I promised you honesty, so here we go. We can start in a week or two. I needed things to quiet down with Simon's... disappearance before heading to *my* unit. Zack had the unit cleaned up so there would be nothing leading back to either of us. I cannot give any more details on his involvement, that's kind of how our friendship works. He's got ties in places that even I will never understand—"

It's as if I can see the thoughts spiraling around his head. I think that's all I'm going to get from him but he doesn't stop.

"In regards to you seeing everything, I do the actual killing and information gathering at a unit that I rent for storage. The bodies, I usually leave them at the last seen location of their last victim." He smiles wide at me, shaking his head, he tucks a single hair behind my ear. "I wanna lie to you so that I don't scare you off. I think no matter what I say, I'll scare you off."

I shake my head, "No, I wanna know the truth. All of it."

Cameron sucks in a breath and shakes his head, "No, baby. I don't feel regrets for killing the people I've killed. I don't even know if I have regrets for when my dad killed your mom. They weren't good people. I feel bad for the pain that it caused you, but they weren't able to hurt anyone else now."

The words, had I heard them the other day, would have sent me into a spiral, but somehow they don't right now. Instead, the settle over me like a piece of me that was missing, that suddenly I'm seeing through a full lens.

"I get it. I think–" My tongue brushes over my teeth, as I try to get the words out that sit heavy in my heart. "I think every-thing upset me as much as it did growing up because I never understood *why* my parents were killed. Now I get it, and now all I want to do is make sure that no one else gets hurt because of people like my parents and Simon."

"Well then, Cherry girl, that's exactly the reason I kept on doing what my dad started. So, if you're ready, we can head to the unit tomorrow morning. We can start your lessons."

His smile matches one of a kid in a candy store and despite the heavy atmosphere, can't help but laugh and smile.

"Let's do this, baby. I'm ready to learn." He pulls me close, pinning me down on the bed. His body hovers over me, leaning down he peppers my neck, chin, and lips with kisses.

"Have I told you how fucking perfect you are?" His voice is a growl and I can't help but let out a gleeful laugh. Cameron hops out of bed, as he pulls me up into his arms.

"Cam! Put me down!" I squirm trying to get out of his arms, but he kisses me again. Relenting he puts me down and slaps my ass. I let out a yelp and reel towards him. "You're such a child!"

He laughs hard as he rolls his eyes, laughing. "Only for my Cherry girl. Only for you." I never want this to end. I will do anything this man tells me to, as long as it means that I will be with him until my very last breath. I interlock my fingers with his, and we start walking back to the front door.

Without warning, he pulls me to a direct stop, his face serious, as he grabs my chin forcing me to keep my eyes on him. I feel the world around me stop, and it's just not fucking fair. "Cam– what is it?" I don't know what to do but my heart stops and I immediately let out a whimper as the fear and tears fly out of me.

He's just staring at me and I start to realize that it's not some sort of inner motivation causing him to stand in my way like this. He's blocking me from seeing something. I try to pull away from his hold, but he only gets firmer. With enough resistance, however, he frees me to not to hurt me. And now I'm staring at it.

Tucked into the frame of his door, sits a single red fucking rose. Before I even have a moment to react, I look towards Cameron, whose brows furrow and without a second thought. "Move in with me."

"I can't breathe, Cameron... I thought–I thought." Cameron grabs my cheeks gently as he firmly grabs me by the chin forcing me to face him.

"Leyla, look at me." His voice is a beacon of calm and confidence. "You are moving in with me. I need to figure out what's happening, and I don't want you anywhere where I can't see you. You are mine, and maybe it wasn't Simon who was leaving you the roses, but I won't let anyone hurt you. I won't let anyone else near you, and you are moving in with me."

The logic is solid, and I know that what he's saying makes sense. I try to look towards the door where the rose sits positioned to taunt me, and his firm grasp doesn't let me.

"No." Cameron practically growls out. "Eyes on me."

A shudder rolls through my body and I can't process what he's saying, but the more that I think about it, the more that this all makes sense. "Okay– okay yea." I sigh and look at him, lips pursed as I start to think of all the logistics of this.

"But... my lease..."

"Let me handle that, we can get you out of this lease because it's no longer safe for you to live here. I'll text Alex if I have to for the legality of all of this. You're safe, baby girl, and I will do everything in my power to make sure that you never feel unsafe again." His hands gently rub up and down my arms, as he has finally dropped his hands from my face. "I love you." Cameron whispers into the crown of my head, and I can't help but melt into him.

30
MOVING TRUCKS
LEYLA

Popping my earbuds in, I press the green call button on Hazel's name. I figure there's no better time than now to tell her all that had happened. I haven't even filled her in on my abduction. I don't think I could ever tell her about what happened with Cameron's dad and my parents, but I think that in some fucked up way, even if I did, it wouldn't even phase her.

Nope, do not. My internal monologue is screaming at me, knowing that I could never tell her.

"LeyLey?" Hazel's panicked voice sounds in my ears and a small smile blooms on my face.

"Hey, Haze–"

"No fucking way, Leyla Joy Clarkson. Don't act cool and casual right now. Where the fuck have you been?! You turned off your location, and I nearly called Detective Alexandra to put out a fucking missing person report on you!" Hazel's voice sounds panicked, and in that moment I know that I can't even tell her about the kidnapping.

It'll only scare her more and I honestly don't know how she would react to something that serious.

Probably try and get me microchipped like a puppy.

"Fuck, Haze, I'm sorry. My phone died, and I've been spending so much time with Cameron that I just never got it off the charger and turned it back on. We made up, and things have been honestly good. Better than good, actually. We talked about everything... And there's something that I wanted to talk to you about."

The line on Hazel's end is silent, and if I didn't hear the crinkle of a blanket just now, I would have honestly thought that she hung up. Her voice was small when she answered, sending a pang of guilt through me.

"Hmm?" The questioning sound hurts me more than it should, but I continue on.

"I'm moving in with Cam."

I know this is probably the worst possible time for all of this seeing as not even 10 days (about 1 and a half weeks) ago he had tried to choke me out during his PTSD attack. Silence on her end. "Hazel?"

Fuck.

"Hazel, please," I plead with her, even though I know that she has every right to be mad at me. Years ago, we promised to always let the other know where we are, what we're doing. Then when tracking came around, the Track My Friends app on my phone is always on, 24/7, knowing that I was always safe, that she would always have my location.

So much for that peace of mind.

"What happened, Leyla?" Her voice is lined with the slightest tinge of anger, but the overarching feeling is pain—and that kills me.

"I walked over to Cameron's house, we talked, we argued a bunch... then we talked some more... Hazel, I know what happened at the rage room was fucked, but I don't blame him for what happened. He wouldn't ever purposely hurt me. He wouldn't purposefully do anything to– and I, I think I'm in love with him."

I do love him. I am in love with him, and I don't know how but right now he is the only thing in my life that truly makes sense. As if on cue, Cameron knocks on the door, a smile on his face as he walks in, nodding as he sees that I'm on the phone.

"Leyla, are you absolutely sure about all of this? This is a really big step." Hazel's logic and trepidation flows through me and honestly, I wish I had it in me to argue, but there is no going around this. I am moving in with him.

"Hazel, it would be a different story had we not been friends growing up. I've known him since I was fourteen, so I know he's a good guy." She knows this, but saying it out loud somehow made it seem more real, more... official. "I'm already almost packed, and my lease is up today anyway. I... I think a change will be good for me." I heard the moment that she realized that I wasn't going to be changing my mind.

"You weren't really friends back then, but fine, fine. Leyla, just please be safe? I don't like this one bit, but you know I love you and just want you to be safe, babes." Hazel's resigned sigh came through, silence pursued. "I love you Leyla, you are my only family, and I need it known that if he ever does anything to you, I will make his life a living fucking nightmare."

The laugh that escapes Cameron's lips, I quickly slap a hand over his mouth— he bites my palm and I hold in a yelp. I really hope she didn't hear that, but I cover it up with a cough.

"Babes, Hazey, I promise you— nothing is going to happen to me. We're good together and though it sounds crazy, we just make sense together."

The silence over the line sends a shift of nerves that I didn't know were there. Cameron gently rubs his fingers over my back, and I lean into him.

"Okay, LeyLey. I still don't like it, but I trust you to be smart." She sighs but I can't help but smile.

"Haze? I love you, like so much."

"I love you too, LeyLey."

I suddenly feel like everything will actually be okay, she approves of us, and it makes me feel so much more confident about all of this.

"Cameron's here now, I'm gonna let you go cause we've gotta finish up with our last-minute packing, okay?" My voice is smoother, the furrow in my brow gone, and my shoulders relaxing even more as I sigh and a shiver runs through me.

"Sounds good, babes. Call me when you get settled?" Her voice is soft, but I think she knows that I wouldn't just jump into something without thinking it through. Cameron and I are truly it, there is no one else, nor would there ever be again for the both of us.

I hang up and put my phone in my back pocket, leaning my head backwards onto Cameron's shoulder. "Hey, baby." His emerald eyes connect with mine, as he places a kiss on the top of my head.

"You almost ready?" Cameron takes a look around the now empty apartment, and the last few remaining boxes. "I got here as quick as I could after work, sorry it took me so long."

"It's okay, I got it all done. And yea, just gotta tape up the last box and then we're all set to bring these last couple boxes down to the truck." My explanation is cut short by his mischievous grin, my eyes open wide.

"I can't believe you're mine. I get you now, all day, every day. You know everything there is to know about me, and you're not scared. You love and accept me for who and what I am, and if that's not the hottest thing–" Cameron nips at my earlobe, a gasp as I lean into him. "You are too good for me, Leyla Joy Clarkson."

I'm almost certain that he feels the moment my heart skips a beat over his words, confirmed by his dark laugh that skitters over the back of my neck. My hair stands up, and I try to push him off. "Cam– I'm all gross and sweaty– *ah!* No– not here!" The laughter carries through the room, he pulls me closer to him, my body instinctively melts into him, tilting my head so that I'm now staring into his incredible eyes that make me just feel all warm and fuzzy inside. I want to fight and push away because I'm tired and gross, but he opens his mouth and I'm simply just putty in his hands.

"That means nothing to me, Cherry. I don't think you know what you fucking do to me." His voice is low and dark, and I watch as his pupils consume the green of his eyes. "I can't wait to christen every single part of our place later." Cameron nips my earlobe again and I let out a soft yelp.

"You've lived there for years, it's not like it's somewhere new," I tease as I turn around in his embrace to face him.

"It's not the same, this is *ours* now. You and me." His fingers interlock with mine and it just for once feels like things are finally going my way and things are looking up. The rest of my life suddenly looks really fucking great, and I don't think I want a single thing to change.

———

The two of us hop in the front seat of the moving truck and all these intense emotions are hitting me that Leyla, after all these years, is truly mine. She's so perfect and I can't help but have a matching smile upon my own face, that somehow has begun living there since we connected again. I turn to look at her, embarrassment etching into her face as she realizes she's been caught staring, my lips twitch upwards as I reach my hand out towards her.

"You okay Cherry Pop?" I give her hand a gentle squeeze, and tilt my head towards her while keeping my eyes on the road.

"Yea baby, I just... So much has happened, and if you would've told me this literally a month ago, I would have laughed at you." Her voice is laced with nerves that are written all over her face, though you can just tell she's trying to keep herself together here, a drastic change from how she was just minutes ago.

"Beautiful, there's nowhere that we wouldn't go that I won't be right by your side. You are my everything, and I promise you that from this day on, I will always keep you safe." I lean over and gently kiss her on the cheek and head off towards the house. *Our* house.

Leyla sits on her phone in the passenger seat, scrolling through social media.

"Holy shit... Is this you?" Leyla holds up her phone to me with the headline reading:

6th Body Found in Maplewood Michigan: is this the Work of The Notorious "Whispering Killer?"

I pinch my brows together trying to read the headline while still keeping my eyes mainly on the road. A deep unsettling feeling sits in the pit of my stomach.

"No, that's not me. My dad– he used to be known as The Whispering Killer. This new killer that they've had all in the news recently has to be a copycat with the same motive as what my dad used to do." I'm sort of ranting at her at this point. Every time I've seen headlines pop up that I know aren't me, my blood kind of boils. While I appreciate having a helping hand out here in the world of cleaning up the trash, they should get their own identity. I shake my head. "I never wanted that name, even though I do exactly what he did."

I'm nothing like that monster. I'm not my father.

"Detective Alex is convinced that this is you." Leyla's voice sounds more timid now. My heart ready to beat out of my own chest thinking about the fact that Detective Alexandra thinks that I am The Whispering Killer. This isn't Leyla's problem, and I'll make sure it stays that way. I'm making a mental note to talk to Zack later and make sure that we scrub the database, checking what information the detective has on me. I turn my attention to Leyla, a placating smile on my lips as I reach for her hand giving it a gentle comforting squeeze.

"How do you know that?" My tone is smooth, betraying nothing of the extreme panic that is now coursing through my body. I keep my face neutral, waiting for her answer. The trees blur by us down the side road as we drive towards the house.

"She started to... Alex started telling me when I met up with her a while ago. And I mean like, she knows The Whispering Killer case better than anyone Cam. She was there from when my parents were killed, and she has been there every step of the way..." I watch her brows stuck knitted together, her chest rising and falling so quickly that it kills me that I'm making her feel this way.

"It's okay. Hey, Cherry– look at me." It takes everything to not pull the car over and pull her into my lap and make sure she knows that she's not alone at this moment. "Breathe with me." I squeeze her hand again as she nods.

"Yea– okay, I can–" Her eyes close and the softness enters her face once again and I feel the air shift again as we continue taking slow breaths together.

"Good girl." My voice comes out more breathy than I intend it to be. I want to hold her, make sure that she knows that she's loved, safe and that I will never let anything happen to her again. Her grip on my hand lessens and I feel so much better seeing that stress fade off her face. "Cherry, I need you to know that nothing bad is going to happen to you ever again. That includes anything with the past. I'm yours, and you're mine."

"Promise?" The trepidation in her voice sends a rush of pain through me, and it makes me realize just how fragile this whole situation is, and what this all means for Leyla.

"I promise you Cherry, forever and always." Giving her hand a gentle squeeze, a small smile forms on her lips giving me the feeling that no matter what happens next, we are forever. She's mine to keep, and I don't plan on ever letting her out of my sight ever again. We will change the world together, and she will be the one to fix the wrongs.

And through it all, she's mine.

31
MISS ME?
THE WHISPERING KILLER

What a fucking joke, does she truly believe that she's safe now? He thinks that he can have her, no questions asked? He had done so well keeping off my radar, we simply existed together. Up until now, his actions have been nothing but a means to an end. I allowed him to work in *my* town.

This is my town, and he's now gotten messy. I can't let them ruin the hard work that I've put into this. Maplewood is a small place, it's all stuck together by fake smiles, secrets, and graves that no one dares dig too deep.

Don't fucking think that I don't remember, I fucking remember it all.

Leyla Clarkson.

I almost felt sorry for her. *Almost.* And pity is not something I allow in often. I heard everything, I know the entire fucking story of how her father was a monster and who he was. Leyla was molded to fit into this story. She's my own story. My place in her life has been cemented since that night, and I don't ever want her to forget her place.

I might be the one hiding in the background, but it's always been me. Do you think she'd ever fucking notice? No. When she was young there were times that I would've been seen as someone who was worth her time. Leyla has a life now. Leyla has someone else who is taking away time that belongs to me.

I walk these streets now, completely invisible. Blending into every crowd, watching from every corner. She passed me just yesterday in town. Her pretty little face tucked beneath a beanie; hand curled around a paper coffee cup like it could protect her. She didn't even flinch when I brushed by her. Not even a flash of recognition that I was the one who saved her all those years ago. All that I had done, *wasted*.

She's lost her instincts.

And *he*— Cameron *fucking* Curtis— thinks he's better than me? Thinks that he's evolved? That because he grew a conscience and fell in love with a girl with broken wings that he's somehow redeemed?

No. You don't get redemption, not in this world.

You take your place, and if you try to rise above it, I bring you back down. I have to teach them who's boss, I have to teach them who's the real killer. I have to teach them who's really in charge here. They don't get that break anymore. My hard work, my good that I've done for the world.

I've got my work cut out for me now, but don't worry this isn't the last you've seen of me. I'm going to give the two little lovebirds a reminder of who's in control here.

32
MILES ON IT
CAMERON

I t's been three months.

My perfect, beautiful Leyla and I have been working towards this incredible moment. Working through the fears and insecurities that come along with the type of things that I do–that *we're* going to do. I stand and watch as she braids her hair, wrapping it up into a bun to keep it off her stunningly sharp features that make this feel so much more finite. We are actually fucking doing this.

Leyla begins pacing slightly as she turns to me, her smile slightly forced, I shouldn't make her do this, she's clearly not ready for this, there's something holding her back.

"You ready, Cherry?" My voice is solid and concise as I look towards her, her shoulders bracketed tight as she stands up straight, stopping her pacing. I lean against the wall of the living room, crossing my legs over the other, watching her with the kind of attention that would make most squirm. She's wearing black— tight, efficient, and all business.

But her hands are shaking. Not much. Barely enough to notice, but I see it. I see everything when it comes to her.

Next, I notice that look on her face— like a scared animal one second, a proud goddess the next. I've always loved that multifaceted way about her, and in the past few weeks that fear has been slowly fading away from her.

"I'm not scared," she lies so easily, a forced nuance but I hear it. And it's not for me, it's for herself. The entire world flashes in her eyes and I don't miss a single second of any of it.

I push off the wall and cross the distance between us slowly, like I'm approaching this wild thing I don't want to scare off. "It's okay if you are," I murmur as I lean into her neck. "The first is one of the most exciting and terrifying things that you could ever go through. Hell, firsts are meant to scare the shit out of you sometimes, but that's how you learn and grow. You get better from fear, but you never let it consume you."

A choked laugh escapes her as she nuzzles into my chest, wrapping her arms around my torso and I pull her into me even closer, not wanting a single part of her to think that she doesn't belong with me.

"I've seen worse," she mumbles into my chest, the words sending vibrations through me.

"I know," I say, softer now. "But watching it happen and making it happen? Planned and not in the heat of the moment? That's a whole different ballgame, Ley."

She exhales hard through her nose, pushing and turning away from me like she doesn't want me to see her breaking. But

I already know, I already see it— and I love her more for it. I may be too far gone, but she isn't there, I won't ever let her break the way that I did. We are meant for each other, and I know that I can keep her innocence and happiness safe. Shaking off the thoughts that are running through my head.

"You remember what he did?" I whisper to Leyla, walking up behind her, needing her closeness for just another moment before we change her life forever.

Leyla swallows deeply and nods slowly. "He drugs girls. Buried one alive."

"Exactly, this isn't someone who deserves to exist anymore. This is someone who has done horrific things to innocent people." My voice is certain and confident, I feel myself slipping into that place that I go to when I have to do this. "Like we practiced, baby. This is going to be easy, and we will be done before you know it."

I see the fear in her eyes as she looks at me, she was so ready just moments ago, but I see the hesitation. The second guessing of her decision to do this with me. But she marinates in my words, getting lost in thought. I let her drift, but I'm here to tether her if she tries to go too far.

Then, Leyla nods. I watch as she prepares herself, her face shutting off the loving, caring, and kind person that I am so in love with, to this woman who is ready to cut the world in half. She takes a couple deep breaths, her eyes squeezing shut. It then hits me that words won't be the answer for Leyla; it won't be enough to center her to do this. I know what I need to do.

"Leyla." My voice is raw, pulling at every single part of me. She whirls to me hearing the gravity of my voice, her pupils block out her beautiful eyes. Leyla's eyes shoot to my hands, as I fall to my knees, holding out the knife in my hand. The silver of the blade glints in the bedroom light, her eyes glinting in understanding what I'm asking her to do. A soft gasp comes from my Cherry, and her face looks even more terrified.

"Cammy... Wh-what are you doing?" I watch as her eyes bounce between me and the knife in my hand.

"I want you to see how much I trust you, okay?" I offer the knife handle towards her, her eyes locked onto mine and her hands shaking. Her brows flick up with recognition as she lets out a whimper as I gently place the knife in her hand.

"I trust you," I assure her.

Leyla's pupils grow wide, but she wraps her fingers around the worn leather handle that means so much to me. She's fucking everything, and there isn't a thing I wouldn't do for her.

33
CUT TO THE CHASE
LEYLA

The knife sits heavy in my hand; it's somehow heavier than it looked in his. Cameron's eyes haven't left mine, burning with a fire that is all consuming. I know we have places to be, a timeline to follow, but he slowly nods, granting access and permission. Taking his shirt off, he shows me his chest as he falls to his knees, the power all in my hands.

A copper tang hitting my tongue as I slip into a mindset that I have been working on with Cameron for months now. "You trust me." I twirl the blade between my trembling fingers, convincing my mind that I'm not nervous. Power isn't something that I've ever been comfortable with, but it's something that I deserve and I know that I want. I fall to my knees gently in front of him, and a grin grows on his face.

"With my life," he whispers. He trusts me with his life— my

heart thumps at the thought. Cameron leans forward, the light glinting off the yellow hues in his green eyes.

"Good, baby." I move the knife towards him, and he doesn't even flinch, doesn't blink. The solid statue in front of me, a dark smile on his face. I slowly place the knife against his throat, his pulse hammering against the blade. I feel the heat everywhere, emanating off of his body, seeping into my bones.

"You should be scared of me," I say as the knife glints, as I drag it down his exposed chest. Tracing the tip of his knife down his sternum, pausing over his heart. His breath catches slightly, heart pounding faster now, his eyes like fire.

"You could gut me right now," Cameron murmurs, a feral growl, his voice rough. "And I'd thank you for it."

"Get on the couch," I command, my voice strong and powerful. I pull the knife away from his heart. Cameron, like the good boy he is, listens to me as he scurries and sits down on the couch. I grin as I straddle him, my hand trembles. Not with fear, but with adrenaline. With *need*.

I can't believe I have this side of me, but now that she's out — she feels right. *I* feel right. This is *me*.

I press the blade against his chest once again; the sharp edge of the knife pressed into his chest. A bead of blood pools up under the press of the knife. He shudders beneath me, and it isn't from fear. It's from restraint.

"You're so fucking good at acting like you're not dying for it," I whisper, dragging the knife sideways now, exploring more of his skin inch by inch down his body.

"I am dying," he says, voice hoarse. "For you."

The words hit me somewhere deep, electric, and primal.

I pressed the knife against his sternum, harder this time— not enough to break the skin, just enough to feel the threat of it —and kissed him. Hard. Bruising.

He kisses me back just as fiercely, teeth clashing, tongues tangling. It's messy and desperate and *real*. I feel his desire flowing through me as our lips rush together. I ground my hips down against his, feeling how much he wants me— and just how close to breaking he is.

My hand grips the knife tighter, dragging the flat of the blade up the side of his neck, over his jaw, my lips following, kissing the trail I left behind. His hands shake where they're gripping the couch cushions, white-knuckled with restraint. I grind my hips against him again, slow and punishing.

I feel Cameron's smile grow against my lips, the knife suddenly forgotten between us. The power dynamic changes in an instant, his hands fly up from where they were on the couch, to where suddenly I'm beneath him, my breasts rising and falling so quickly from the pure adrenaline flowing between us. His body looms over me, urgent and strong.

"I got you," he purrs, a growl as his eyes rove over my body, a dark promise in them. My breath catches as he grabs the knife from my hands. Using the tip of the knife, he gently pushes hair off my face.

His mouth crashes down on mine once again, savage and claiming. He kisses me like he's trying to devour me, biting my bottom lip hard enough that I am suddenly tasting the metallic tang of blood— *my* blood— and it only makes me hotter.

Cameron's hands are everywhere; gripping, bruising, worshiping. He broke the kiss just long enough to yank my shirt over my head, tossing it somewhere across the room without a care.

"You're fucking mine," he growls into my neck, and I whimper pathetically, arching into him.

His hips grind down, hard and fast, rubbing against the ache building between my thighs. My body moves instinctively, chasing the friction, chasing him. His hands slide down my sides, rough and possessive. He fumbles with the button on my jeans, yanking them down with a force that has me gasping for air. Cool air hit my thighs, and then his hand is there— hot, demanding— sliding between my legs. I cry out when his fingers plunge into my underwear, finding me wetter than I've ever been. Cameron lets out another pained growl, low and vicious, like he might tear me apart if I don't let him in imme-diately.

"Cam—" I beg, but it's useless. He already knows. He shoves his jeans and boxers down enough to free his cock, then grabs my hips, holding me still as he lines up his huge cock. I barely have time to breathe before he thrusts into me in one hard, brutal stroke.

I *scream*— a broken, desperate sound— and he swallows it with a kiss. He moves fast, rough, fucking me like he was trying to bury himself inside me, to brand me from the inside out.

Every thrust knocks the breath from my lungs, my nails claw at his back, and I leave angry red lines across his skin.

"Cherry," he groans against my mouth, voice wretched. "Fuck." *Thrust.* "You feel so good." *Thrust.* "So fucking perfect —" *Thrust.*

I couldn't think.

Could barely *breathe.*

All I knew was Cameron. Cameron slamming into me, Cameron's teeth biting down on my shoulder hard enough to leave bruises, Cameron's hands holding me down like I might float away without contact. There is only *Cameron.* I meet every thrust of his, wildly and frantic, together we're dangerous, like we're going to fly off the cliff any moment.

"Cam– *fuck.*" I feel my orgasm building and reaching its peak in a monumental frenzy, broken sobs sounding from my lips as it rips through me like lightning. My back arches off the couch, my thighs trembling against his hips. Cameron lets out a feral growl as he slams into me once, twice more before following with a shuddering orgasm inside me.

He collapses onto me, his breaths hard. He smiles softly as he presses his forehead against mine. For a moment, all the world is just fading away. I thread my fingers through his now sweat-soaked hair, pulling him closer.

"Mine," I whisper against his swollen lips.

His bright and satiated eyes connect with mine, he looks up at me and whispers back, "Always."

We sit there for a few minutes more, quietly, coming down from the probably most phenomenal orgasm of my entire life. His voice breaks the silence. "You ready to change the world, Cherry?"

It hits me then that I no longer feel that fear that was eating at me only a little while ago. This man is my fucking hero, and my undoing.

"Yea Cam. Let's do this." A grin creeps up onto my face, "But maybe a shower first." I relent, his laugh soft as he nods.

"Of course, let's go."

"Of course, let's go."

34
TEAR THEM DOWN
LEYLA

I hop in the shower, letting the sweat and sex rinse off me. Cameron joins me, his finger gently tracing over my blossoming bruises that he left on me in our crazy tangle.

"You're a fucking animal," I chuckle as he traces over a particularly sensitive bruise.

"Only for you, Cherry." Cameron's voice is teasing as I turn off the water, carefully stepping out of the shower, with him following close behind me. "We're leaving in ten minutes, okay?"

I nod and kick myself into gear and throw on tight black leggings and a black shirt. Making my way into the kitchen, I wrap my hand around my favorite mug that I quickly fill with tap water and take a sip, waiting for Cameron to finish getting ready. As if on cue he walks up behind me, purring, "Cherry." His hands, warm and calloused, wrap around my waist, anchoring me to something solid. "You ready?"

I nod and let a soft smile on my face. I try not to think about what we're doing, but the gravity of it still sits in my chest. I turn around in his comforting grasp, my eyes connecting with his. I nod again, my eyes flying to the knife, that was mine for just a fantastic moment, I see tucked into the belt on his pants.

He pulls away from me and for a second, I hate the lack of his touch. He presents a smaller knife and my eyebrows shoot up with shock when I realize that it's for me. I gently grab the blade from his hands, examining it. "For me?"

A boyish smile dominates his face that sends a thrill through me, and he laughs. "Yea, Cherry girl, I wanted something for you. One that's yours and that you could see belongs to you. Only you can control what this knife does. Understand?"

I nod, "Yea."

"Good. Let's go." Both of our demeanors shut down, changing so quickly as we head to his car in preparation for what's to come. This is what I've trained for— I'm ready. Twisting my red hair back, my eyes cooling to shards of ice as I look at Cameron. I'm not a victim, I'm not a scared little girl.

Now, I am a weapon.

———

The drive to the spot to ditch the car is quiet, both of us in our own heads, preparing and nothing else. He parks and pulls out his balaclava, and hands me one as well. Cam gets out of the car, moving to my side to open the door for me, and offers me his leather gloved hand.

The night swallows us whole as we step outside. Our boots

quiet against the sidewalk as we walk towards the garage of the man we're going to take care of tonight. Our pace quickens as we make our way towards the end of the small street, our bodies a simple shadow in the night.

The garage looms ahead, a crooked skeleton against the gray sky.

He's inside.

Waiting.

Though he doesn't know it yet.

Cameron gestures, two quick flicks of his fingers, and I follow without hesitation. My pulse thrums in my throat, not with fear but with focus. Every breath, every heartbeat, every step steels me even more. We sneak through the broken doorway, careful not to disturb the shards of glass scattered like glitter across the floor.

That's when the stench of the garage hits me. *Rot.* Oil. Something worse beneath it all.

Cameron's shoulder brushes mine, grounding me, and together we slip into the shadows.

That's when this all becomes real because there he is. It's funny we spent so much time preparing for this— *a flashback to the hot summers in Daddy's garage.* Well, that's an unwelcome memory that I quickly shake off; my past has no right to fucking come back and torment me right now. I focus back into the moment, Cameron's emerald orbs trained on me for a moment.

My eyes lock on the man in front of us, he's honestly fucking huge, so much bigger than he was in the pictures. He sits on a rusty chair, greasy hands on a tool tightening something on an old car. This man has no idea that these are the last moments of his pathetic life.

I stand there, just watching him breathe. My eyes flick over to Cameron, a quiet question sitting in his eyes. *You or me?* His gaze never leaving mine, a smirk in the shadows sits across his lips visible through his mask.

My smile echoes his, a dark sinister part of me ready to make a change. *Us.*

I make the first move, and the knife is already in my hand as I close the distance.

He doesn't even realize I'm there until my blade kisses the skin at his throat. He jerks, startled, but it's too late—Cameron's behind him in an instant, shoving him back down into the chair with a rough hand on his shoulder.

"Don't scream," I whisper against his ear, the blade pressing deeper. "Or you'll die before we have our fun."

The prick freezes. The scent of fear pours off him in waves, thick enough to choke on. I glance at Cameron. He nods once, and the real work begins.

I let the tip of my knife dance along his jawline, slow, playful, cruel. I want him to feel all of it, I want him to *know* what's coming. "You remember Jenna Lewis?" I murmur, barely above a breath.

The man's body stiffens under my blade. I can't help but let a smile escape knowing that this is a good thing now, he does fucking remember. With what this piece of shit has done to other women, what he did to Jenna, he honestly fucking deserves so much worse than what Cameron and I are going to do to him.

Cameron crouches beside him, unfolding a worn photograph— the kind the news forgot a long time ago. A girl with too-wide eyes and a smile that never stood a chance.

"You buried her alive," Cameron says, voice low and lethal. "Now you get to feel what she felt." David tries to struggle, he tries to fight back, but Cameron pins him like it's nothing. Like he's swatting a fly. Holy *fuck* is that hot.

I press the flat of my blade against his cheek, watching the tears form at the corners of his eyes. "You're not getting out of this," I whisper. "No begging. No mercy."

I slice.

Not deep.

Just enough to bleed.

His scream is muffled by Cameron's hand, and I feel the rush of it hit me like a shot of adrenaline straight to the heart. I meet Cameron's eyes over our victim's trembling head. He's smiling— smiling like a man who has everything he's ever wanted right in front of him. And maybe he does. Maybe *we both do.*

Because this? This is where we belong. Covered in blood. Breathing violence like it's oxygen. Feeling alive in a way that no soft, safe life could or would ever offer.

Together.

Over the next hour, we finish what we came to do. Cameron pulls out a burner phone that he had stashed away, sending out a text to someone who I can only assume would be Zack, who

I've learned over the past few weeks is a cleaner, hacker and part of some Motorcycle club. The dude sounds fucking terrifying, and I genuinely hope that I never have to meet him. Cameron smiles as we finish up and head back to his car.

We just killed someone, and I don't feel the slightest bit bad about it.

35
FALSE CONFIDENCE
CAMERON

I look towards Leyla as she stands at the stove, the smell of bacon sneaking its way through the house. Since having Leyla move in, we've fallen into this routine, and even the woman who swore up and down that she would never be the one to cook, is standing at my stove, wearing my "kiss the chef" apron, her red hair tied up in a ponytail.

It's been six months since she moved in with me and I honestly wouldn't change it for a thing.

"What do we have on the books today, baby?" She turns her head towards me, a soft smile on her face that makes her radiate more than the morning sun. I almost don't respond because I'm so enamored with my girl.

"Huh? Oh, we've got a meeting with Alex today about nailing down some final loose ends with the program. I think we're meeting her at the diner at..." I look down at my phone, scrolling through our calendar. "Four-thirty. Which meaaaans." A devilish grin forms on my face, as she lets out a pained groan.

"You're relentless." Her sing-songy voice lilts through the somewhat noisy kitchen, but it floats above it all.

I can't help but laugh. "Fine, fine. I was gonna head by the storage locker for some last-minute work if you'd like to join me?" I can't help but sit at our little island, just truly in awe of this woman. Leyla plates up the bacon, eggs and what looks to be like a hash brown casserole, which I watched her pull out of the oven with ease. "This all smells delicious baby, thank you for making breakfast."

She sets the plates out and I watch with rapt attention. This woman is so fucking incredible, I can't help but have the dumbest smirk on my face. Leyla sits down next to me, and I lean over and kiss her cheek as I take a bite of the food she prepared. She looks at me through her thick lashes, a sinful smirk on her face.

"I hope you like it! I worked really, *really* hard on it."

I stab some food onto my fork and shovel it into my mouth. The immediate taste of burnt bacon overtakes my tastebuds. I let out a quick cough and plaster a smile on my face. "W-Wrong pipe!" I quickly try to cover up the intense overly spiced flavors that attack my mouth.

Her face looks so hopeful, and I don't have it in me to hurt her feelings. Maybe the hashbrowns are going to be better, so I take another bite this time of those and somehow, they are both under and overcooked at the same time. I chew carefully with a smile on my face. "Wow, baby, you're fucking amazing, is there anything you can't do?" I take a sip of my coffee and silently thank the gods for the reprieve from whatever the hell she just made for me.

"You like it?!" She gleams so brightly towards me, the pride beaming off of her. "I was so nervous that you wouldn't like it. It's my first time making it!"

"No, Cherry, you're fucking amazing. I'm so proud of you." Never once actually saying that it was her food that was good, one less mark on my soul, a small diversion, but one that I know she needs.

Leyla smiles as she goes to take a bite of her creation, and her face instantly falls, as she spits out the food right back onto her plate.

"That's fucking terrible!" she squeals as she chugs her water, trying to get the taste out of her mouth. "Cameron Michael Curtis! You fucking liar!" She playfully hits my chest, losing my balance as I nearly fall off the stool, catching myself on the counter before I do.

"Hey! That was uncalled for! I never lied!" I'm trying my absolute hardest to not lose my absolute shit in a fit of laughter. I can't tell if she's upset or also trying to keep it together too. "I said *you're* amazing...this is..." I hold up the poorly cooked hash-brown casserole and give out an exasperated chuckle.

"It's absolute crap! Oh my god! How can I ever believe you again?!" Leyla's face is both upset and sympathetic. "I'll order us food– I'm literally so sorry." She tries to take my plate away and toss it in the trash and I grab her wrist, my voice taking a dark tone.

"I'm not done eating." Realizing that she thinks that she messed up does something to my heart. This woman has turned me so soft, and with a sort of defiance that I know I'll regret, I take another bite of her food.

"Oh my god! Cameron, please! This is literally not edible!" Her pleading voice fills me with such joy, that old Cameron would never have thought that he would have deserved.

"No, you worked so hard to make this." I motion to the set up of all the food in front of us with my free hand, my other around her wrist.

"Baby, you don't have to prove anything to me, I know that I made all of this for you but I'm almost certain that if you eat anymore of this you will literally die from undercooked eggs or something." She presses her entire body up against me, gently kissing along my jaw; the kiss is tender enough to be an apology all on its own.

"I love you so much, Cameron, but I am asking you to please not eat this. Don't make me beg you," her voice vibrating against my cheek. I let out a soft laugh and turn towards her and gently place a kiss on her soft lips.

"I love you too. Plus, I think I know the best way you can make it up to me." My brow quirking as she looks down at my straining cock, my gray sweatpants pitched with the clear reaction to what my girl does to me. "Do you see what you do to me, Cherry? How is a man supposed to survive when just looking at you has me fucking at attention instantly."

Leyla tips her head back, a true and gentle laugh escaping from my girl's lips. "Oh my god, Cameron."

"On your knees, baby girl." My voice is dark and gravelly, as my hands help guide her down. Looking down at Leyla as she drops to her knees instantly, her eyes wide and her body ready like the good little slut she is.

Her eager hands are pulling at the waistband of my pants, I help her out and the pants fall around my ankles. My cock springing up pressing up against my stomach. She licks her delicious lips as she takes me in as if it's a meal she can't wait for. Her teeth bite into her pillowy lower lip, as she looks up at me. Precum already forming at the head of my cock.

"Tell me what you want baby girl." My voice comes out barely human, a growl. Seeing my girl on her knees for me sends my cock twitching. I'm about to fucking come apart, like an inexperienced schoolboy. She hasn't even touched me yet. I grab her by the base of her neck, gripping the back of her neck, yanking her head back by her hair.

"Suck," my voice is firm and commanding, a feral grin sitting on my face as she licks her lips once again. The bratty gleam in her eyes flickers for a second before fading into soul consuming lust.

She nods quickly, and in a second her lips wrap around the tip of my cock. My hips buck as she does— the slightest touch from her sends a rush of immense pleasure through me. I need to hold it together. I want to enjoy this, savor it, memorize it, etch it onto the fabric of my mind like scripture.

My fingers knot in her hair as her tongue rolls down my shaft and licks in intoxicating swirls as if she's writing the ways of pleasure in cursive. And when she hits the base of my cock, Leyla's cheeks hollow from the suction she provides.

She is worshiping at my altar, and I am a loved and revered God if her mouth is her act of devotion. She's devouring me, body and soul as she sucks, licks, and hums around me. Everything has melted away but the two of us, and there is only this moment with her.

"Good girl," I manage to purr. "Just like that."

My hand guides her head as she takes me in long strokes, the tip of my cock gliding against the velvety interior of her throat. When I push myself deeper, I feel her gag and I start to pull back— but her nails dig into my thighs. My girl continues to gag and squirm as she takes all of me into her mouth and throat. Both of us are covered in her spit and her eyes are watering from the intensity of it— but she looks so fucking determined.

I hear myself panting before I register that I am. Forcing her to slow with my grip in her hair, I blissfully edge for a moment. I'm on the brink of ecstasy, balls deep in the mouth of the woman I love, and she looks as though her very reason for breathing is to do this. I want to live inside this moment, but my body can't take anymore pleasure without relief.

"You're going to swallow for me, aren't you, baby girl? Swallow for me," I say breathlessly.

Without hesitation, she quickens her movements and sucks even harder. I come so hard that it takes my body a full minute to roll through the initial shockwave of it. My hips are pumping against her face and moving her head with a bit of force as I fuck her mouth through every delicious wave and tingle.

Finally, I let her go and Cherry is sitting up, her mouth glistening and her eyes wicked. So much for all those thoughts about being a worshiped God, for right now and forevermore, I would move worlds if that's what she asked of me.

36
I FOUND
LEYLA

"Alex! Hi!" I smile widely as Cameron and I walk into the diner, Alex has a bright smile on her face. She ushers me into a tight hug. I melt into her embrace as she tightens her arms around me. I play the part as if nothing's wrong.

Cameron's face is slightly stoic like it normally is around people that aren't me, Zack, or now Hazel. A practiced smile sits on his face as he nods a greeting towards Alex. "Hey Alex, how are you?"

Alex's smile doesn't falter as she lets go of me and turns her attention to Cameron. "I'm good. Things have been really busy, with work and starting up the program. But it's all going to be worth it, you know? Making the world a better place."

She motions for Cameron and I to sit down at the table she's been holding until we arrive. Clearly, she has everything all set up and ready for us as there's manila folders in piles and a notebook with her chicken scratch in front of her spot at the table. "Sorry for the mess, but please– sit. Let's talk."

A sudden unsettling feeling settles over me. I shake it off as the three of us claim our seats at the table. It's been six months since I received the last rose from... whoever it is. Maybe it was already there before Simon— no he was already dead by the time we got home, and we would have seen it upon arriving. We were inside when the rose was left.

Cameron's hand gently lands on my knee, a soft grounding factor that has become my constant. Cameron squeezes my leg, a silent question and answer all in one. I put a smile on my face and turn my full attention towards Alexandra now.

"Okay, so we're a few months from opening day, where are we now?" Cameron's confident voice takes the lead of this entire conversation. The energy at the table still isn't sitting right with me. I don't quite know what's happening, but I feel anxiety starting to crawl just under my skin.

My intuition is screaming like sirens in the back of my head.

Alexandra smiles as she runs her hand through her raven hair, her smile a bright contrast. "Well, we've got thirty-two adults currently signed up for the program itself. Myself at the helm here, and you two helping with locations and plans for at least the first year. I had Simon scouting out locations for some of them, and another kid from your year in group, Ryann helping out on the business and marketing aspect of it. Simon however had some... personal stuff come up. He sent a text a few months ago saying that he had to head home to take care of personal matters."

I cock my head slightly as if I was just simply reacting to

her. "Oh! That's sad. I haven't heard from him in a couple months, either. Well, I'm happy to help with some of the other locations since he hasn't gotten back to you."

"Yea, it came as a bit of a surprise to me seeing as he was so motivated to help with this project, and it's not like him to just disappear with no notice. But, I digress. And thank you, I'd appreciate some help from you." Alex's intense gaze tears me apart as we sit at the table.

"How's the family?" Alex asks Cameron, the question slightly catching me off guard seeing as I'm pretty sure Alex is more than aware that Cameron's dad is dead. "Anything new and exciting with your father?"

Cameron's face blanches, talking about his father is not something that he does often, even around me and I know him better than anyone. I don't know how to even respond to that question; it seems so out of place for the detective. My hand instinctively now heads to his knee and I sigh softly.

Trying to get Alex's gaze on myself instead, even though Alex's gaze burrows into Cam. I can see his shoulders slumping out of the corner of my eye; he's trying so fucking hard to not show any reaction to her question. He's already been on edge as it has been lately, I've not been much better.

"I thought you'd have heard, my father died last year. Dementia got him in the end, and he passed in his sleep. The only other family I've got now is Leyla, and she and I are closer than ever. Thanks for asking." The rehearsed phrase makes my heart crack just a little more every day, his tone is clipped and short.

The two of them have a sort of stare off that sends a shiver down my spine. I don't know what happened in such a short amount of time, but somethings off. I can't help but think back to Alex's conversation with me months ago that she thinks Cameron was The Whispering Killer.

That impending doom settles in on my chest again, and I give Cameron a look that isn't returned. I know what a trigger Cameron's dad is to him, and I can see him shutting down. I know how hard he works to not let his father's looming memory get the best of him, but clearly that's not in the cards today.

"Well, as fun as this has been, I'm exhausted. I've got a paper due tomorrow, and I really think we should head home," I say after what seemed like an eternity, effectively breaking this silent pissing contest the two of them decided to have right here.

"Yea, of course, Cherry. Let's go." Cameron stands abruptly. Alex looks as though she's going to say something to stop us, but Cameron holds out his hand to her. "Have a great day. We will definitely be in touch about locations for the group. Talk soon."

My hand finds his, and he grips my hand tighter as we head out quickly to the car. His hulking body lumbering behind me like a zombie.

His body is practically vibrating with rage and an emotion that I can't quite pinpoint. I haven't seen him this way for a while now. "Baby... Hey, look at me." I gently press him up against his car. "Come back to me."

I'm careful not to trigger him, my body is just close enough to him that he feels my presence. "Cameron, look at me." I know that if I touch him, it could backfire on me and I could end up with his hand around my throat. His eyes seem far off and distant, but I'm not afraid. I'm never afraid of him. He may be standing still, but his chest is rising and falling at a rate that I know isn't good.

"Cammy." I stand up on my tiptoes and whisper in his ear, our childhood nickname, my one standing defense against the monsters in his mind. "Cammy, you're safe. Look at me. Look at your Cherry." I gently push off his car, my arms around him, though still not touching.

"Hey, there you are." It's subtle, but it's a flicker of his eyes towards me. I see him, the man I love coming back to me. "Hey you." I coo softly, as he looks towards me now. Gently raising my hands, I cup his cheek, and he instinctively leans into my touch.

"I'm sorry," he whispers, his voice hoarse as if he's been screaming, though he hasn't said a word.

"Shh, none of that, baby." I stand up taller and gently kiss his nose. "I love you. Gimme the keys, I'll drive us home," I say softly, holding out my hand. Expecting Cameron to fight back, he hesitantly places the keys in my hand, and I walk him over to the other side of the car and he gets in silently.

The entire car ride home is void of conversation, his hand never leaving mine as we make our way there. I park and get us inside where immediately I lead him to our bed; without question, he crawls in and closes his eyes. Whatever monsters my love faces when it comes to his father, they have him in this chokehold. I want to protect him from it. I will do anything to make this man that I love so much, feel the same amount of love that he's always given to me.

His vibrating body instantly softens when I place my hand on his back.

"You and me, Cammy. I've got you." My voice floats over to him in barely a whisper. A soft smile appears on his face. "I love you."

37
TEAR DOWN THE HOUSE
CAMERON

Leyla had to talk me down again; I've been losing myself a little bit more every day and I feel like I'm going crazy. The air around us changed since the other night. Leyla's asleep on the couch as I pace around the bedroom, trying to rationalize what the fuck is going on right now. I'm losing control and I don't like it.

A sudden ringing cuts through the quiet like a blade. I snatch the phone off the nightstand, heart already beating faster when I see Zack's name. My eyes flick towards Leyla's sweet and peaceful body, her chest rising and falling as if there's not a care in the world. Good.

I'm at least doing something right.

He doesn't call unless it's serious. Not anymore, it's encrypted messages only. He's smarter than that but with the loss of control of everything, I can't help but feel the impending sense of utter fucking dread surging through my veins like sludge, catching on every crevice, and leaving darkness all in its wake.

"Yeah?" I answer, already on edge. My fingers clench my phone tighter than normal, my knuckles turning white.

"You need to listen to me, and don't say anything until I'm done," he says. His voice is sharp, low, like someone could be listening even from where he is— miles away, across state lines. I feel my legs ready to give out from underneath me. *Fuck.*

I know better, I don't say a word.

"I got a ping," Zack says. "Old contact of mine in law enforcement. Not local. He says the detective pulled your name. Leyla's, too. There are surveillance orders out. She's having you watched."

I stand up, the floor cold under my feet grounds me for a moment. My gaze falls to Leyla's sleeping form once again; she's safe, she's right here.

"What the hell do you mean she pulled our names?"

"I mean she's making it official. She's not just sniffing around anymore, Cam. The bitch is building something. Or trying to."

My eyes dart to the window. The street outside is empty, but it suddenly feels too quiet. Manufactured. Like someone's waiting for movement.

"Did your tip give you any inclination as to what Alex is after?"

"No. Just that she's pushing harder. And that you and Leyla are being followed— nothing major, just patterns. Cameras. Unmarked cars. Eyes."

I run a hand through my hair. "Leyla's been restless.

Jumpy. I thought it was just... everything catching up to her. I-I haven't been good lately either, Z. I nearly lost my shit yesterday, had a whole ass panic attack in the diner parking lot."

"Now you know why."

"*Shit*, that fucking motherfucker," I mutter, running my hand through my already mussed hair. Silence stretches between us, thick with all the things we can't say out loud.

"You need to be smart, C," Zack adds. "Don't get paranoid. Don't do anything that gives her an excuse to close in. She's obviously waiting for you two to make a mistake." Zack's tone sends me for a loop. I know he's seen some shit, but for a second there, I almost thought I heard a hint of emotion.

I nod, even though he can't see me. "We'll handle it."

"You'd better. Because if Alex is watching, it's not because she's fucking bored. I'm pretty sure it's because she's onto something. That woman just doesn't fucking know when to stop. I've been keeping tabs on her since you asked me to. She'd been quiet for a bit. Looked you up once or twice."

A cold shutter hits me as a dark realization dawns on me. "Z, could you see that her search history about me... or about my dad?"

"I'm almost insulted, kid. Of course I can. What exactly are you looking for? Any key words?" Zack's voice is just as monotone and unmoving as ever, I don't know how I ever got so lucky, but he is the closest thing to an actual brother I've ever had.

"One, I'm not a kid, I'm only four years younger than you." I hear a snort on the other line, the only break in the man's shut down facade. "Two, anything about my dad? Alex mentioned him, well she asked how my family was."

The memory of the way the woman's eyes burrowed into my psyche sends another whole-body shiver through me.

"Give me a second." I hear a clattering of keys and clicks, a sharp inhale of his breath. "She looked up Michael about two weeks ago, the obituary website being the site she clicked on and stayed on the longest."

A soft hand startles me; I had been so focused on Zack's call I didn't even hear Leyla sneak up on me. She sits down on the bed next to me.

"What's going on?" she whispers, her brows furrowed in concern as she pulls me to a sitting position on the bed.

"Hey, Hack," Leyla says sweetly as she grabs the phone from my hand, putting the phone on speaker.

"Hey, Slice." Zack's voice softens just slightly when he speaks to my Leyla. I turn my attention to her and run my hands through my hair again.

"Alexandra is having us followed."

The words slip out of my mouth before I have a chance to think about what to tell her. All of this is getting too fucking real now, and it's all coming crumbling down around me and I can't take this anymore.

Leyla sighs, "Well, what does she know, Hack? Is this something that we have to be super worried about? I've never been involved in something like this before, and I don't know what to do about any of this. This is all new to me." Leyla's voice is so steady and certain that this pillar of a woman, who was so broken, is suddenly the one taking care of me in this.

Zack lets out a mirthful chuckle, "Well, I recommend y'all take a break for a bit. Keep things low key. Don't do what y'all do. Go on a vacation. Lover's trip or some shit like that. Just be— normal."

"Thanks, Z. Talk soon."

I cut the phone call short, my emotions are already running rampant. I barely know what's happening anymore but it all hits me, that Detective Alexandra could be the death of, well not just me anymore, the death of us. We won't survive this if she keeps this up.

"What if we killed her?" My voice sounds gravelly as I look at Leyla, who's looking at me like I've finally lost it; it's the first time she's ever looked at me that way.

"Cammy, are you really sure that's the best idea right now?" Her voice, her face are all terrified, but for the first time in weeks I finally have this sort of clarity that had been avoiding me for so long.

My eyes connect with the woman who I fucking love so much; she has made my life complete. Maybe Zack is right, maybe we should take a trip away just the two of us.

Leyla pulls me close to her, she pulls me close to everything that I know of safety and she kisses me. "I'm so sorry, Cameron."

I pull back almost shocked; I don't honestly know in what world she thought that she would ever need to apologize.

"I'm gonna call Hazel, just to let her know we're going on a little vacation, okay?" Leyla pulls me close to her again. Kissing my cheek, she hops up and pulls her phone out calling Hazel.

38
KISS ON A ROSE
THE WHISPERING KILLER

Do you know what's so funny about fear? Do you know how easy it is for fear to just wholly consume someone? They don't fucking know how good they had it. They don't know how simple things could be for them if they did not fucking take what belonged to me. Who do they think they are?

Fear is what will be the death of them. His face when I left the note and the flower, was too perfect. The blood draining from his face was something that I never thought I'd ever actually see.

Like the petals had whispered his name.

Maybe they did. I was careful, I had taken my time. Left it just where it needed to be. On the hood of the car, not the windshield. Something about that would've been too obvious, too ordinary. No, this had to be done the right way. *Personal.*

They got too close. I had to knock them down a peg. I knew

that watching the two of them. The added eyes only made my work that much easier. I've always had the upper hand. They just didn't see it before. But now they're starting to. Now they feel it in every quiet moment, every shadow that moves around them just a little too fast. That's what I have to do. I take their silence, and I whisper their names into it. I remind them they're not alone.

They thought they were hunting me. That's cute.

They don't understand that this was never their game to play. It's mine. And I'm not done. Not until I take back what's mine— every heartbeat they stole, every lie they wrapped in sugar and smiles. They reached into my world and took something that belonged to me.

Now I'm going to tear them apart.

Fear will be their downfall. Not violence. Not blood. No— just the knowledge that I'm still out there, watching. Closer than they think.

This isn't my final act, but I need them to know that nothing they do will ever keep them safe. Not from me.

39
YOU'RE LOSING ME
CAMERON

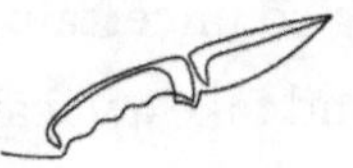

Leyla opens our front door, a greasy brown paper bag in her hand, the most beautiful smile on her face. This woman is my absolute rock. "I grabbed us some lunch, baby." Her slender body coming up to me, leaning up on her tiptoes to kiss my cheek. I can't help but smile back down at her.

"I'm not–" even before I can reply her finger flies up to my lips effectively shutting me up. My lips quirks up in a gentle smile knowing full well that she's truly it for me.

"Nope!" Leyla grins back at me, her face morphing into a smirk. She knows exactly what she's doing, as she pulls me away from my suitcase, dragging me over to the island, and sits me down. "Baby, you need to eat. So, eat."

The brown paper bag plops down in front of me, though it's Leyla's soft floral scent that wraps me up like a warm hug. I can't help but chuckle knowing how absolutely down bad I am for her. She perches on the stool next to me and passes out the burgers and fries.

"I love you," I smile softly.

"I love you too, baby."

Leyla smiles even wider towards me. We fall into a content silence, and I can't help but picture how the rest of our lives will play out. We won't ever stop being who we are, doing what we do, but with things being so uncertain, we both decided to take a break from all of this, and take a vacation.

"You finished packing?" I ask as I take a bite of the burger. She smiles back at me, her stunning eyes shimmering in the sunlight that streams through the window.

"All packed and ready to go. I really cannot wait to go to Pennsylvania! I've never been!" She beams as conversation just flows between us; it's like nothing is ever going to change between us. "When are we heading out?"

Her head tilts with a question. The question something that I've been contemplating as well. I know that we don't have the biggest window of when this would make sense for us to go, but I smile softly.

"We're heading out as soon as we're done eating, I wanna hit the road before it gets too dark. Plus, I think I saw that there was a storm heading in, so I wanna get ahead of it."

I finish eating and lean my arms onto the counter, just admiring the woman that I am so fucking in love with.

Cleaning up, we leave the place spotless for when we get back— there's nothing worse than leaving a mess for yourself in the future. I grab my suitcase and duffle and set it all by the door. I'm so ready for this, I am so ready to take a step back and finally begin this part of my life with the woman that I love.

Leyla pads out of the bathroom, her face lit with unending joy and genuine excitement. The look on her face is something that I will stop at nothing to keep there now. I open my arms to her, she walks briskly into them, and my arms wrap around her, my head pressing into her hair. I inhale deeply and her scent fills my nostrils with this unending sense of home.

"Ready, Cherry?" I whisper into the top of her head, her head leaning up to look at me. She nods gently and pushes off of me.

"Ready, Cammy. Let's go have some real fun for once." Leyla's hand lands on the top of her suitcase, the other shoots out and our hands interlock. We take one more deep breath and then head out the door on what will be an incredible trip that we both need in our souls.

40
NO

ZACK

It's not as if I'm not used to Cameron going off grid. He's done this before, and we've always had a plan in place for when he's going off radar. I know the two of them were heading off the grid, and that's all I know. I hardly sleep as it is these days, with everything going on with Sam– but that's neither here nor there.

I scour my computer for something, literally anything. His fucking obsession with his old ass car, not having a low jack on it. His phone is dead, even his emergency phone. Leyla was with Cameron, so I know that he'd fucking cover his tracks, and all this is doing for me is fucking with my already fucked sleep schedule. I even scour Hazel's phone; she hasn't heard a single thing from Leyla or Cameron either.

I try to make my way into Leyla's phone to see what was going on before she turned it off, or it died. The two of them last pinged in Pittsburgh. Their last known location was the last fucking thing on my mind, thinking that something could happen to them, but I won't let myself go there yet. I'm shocked out of my thoughts by the buzzing of my personal phone.

An unknown number.

Except if it's Cam or even Slice now, I never answer it on the first call. The phone rang once. Then again. And again. I let it go to voicemail.

A bell chimes on my computer. I broke through her phone's wall at last, and I immediately begin to scour through it, raking through the information. A shallow intake of breath sounds from me when my phone starts to fucking ring again. I open her messaging app, that's when it blinks onto the screen—

Leyla's last message was just three words: **We're not safe.**

"Hello?" My resolve is set in place, unmoving as I keep things one level. "Who is this?"

"Hi there, my name is Detective Hall from the Pennsylvania State Police. I'm sorry to call so early, but— is this Mr. Blake? Zackary Blake?" The woman's voice on the other end is clipped, short, but professional. Clearly not the first time the woman's making a phone call like this.

My stomach drops. I fucking know that something is wrong, and I damn well know what this woman was about to say. I let my guard down just slightly. "What happened?"

There is a pause. She is carefully deciding her words. I could hear it. I could fucking hear it in the way her voice softens slightly, like that made anything she was about to say easier.

"There was an incident reported earlier this morning," she says. "A vehicle matching the description of the car registered to Cameron Curtis was found abandoned and burned off a rural road outside Fox Chapel Cliffs."

My entire world tilts.

"Burned?" I repeat to the woman like I didn't understand English.

"Yes," she says hesitantly. "I'm very sorry to inform you... there were human remains inside. A male and a female. Both burned beyond visual identification. But the license plate matches the vehicle registration for the vehicle Cameron Curtis and Leyla Clarkson were last seen in."

I can't speak. Can't breathe. What the fuck did those two get themselves into this time? I told them not to fucking do anything stupid, not to attract any unnecessary attention to themselves.

"I know this is difficult," the woman on the other end of the line continues, "but we'll need someone to provide dental records or DNA, in case the medical examiner can't make a definitive match."

"No," I say. It comes out fast. Reflexive. "It's not them. You said you couldn't ID the bodies." As Leyla's last messages come back to the front of my mind.

We're not safe.

"Seeing as you were listed as Mr. Curtis's next of kin, and Leyla had Mr. Curtis listed as hers, we aren't sure of who else to contact. We are very sorry to tell you this, but Cameron and Leyla are dead. We will be investigating, but it just seems as though the two of them were in a car accident, and the car itself caught fire. If it's any consolation, it doesn't seem like either of them had survived the initial crash before the fire."

I don't think I am actually hearing a fucking word this woman says to me. She continues with things that I probably should be paying attention to. My world begins to fragment, and I don't know what comes over me, the man of logic and data.

"They're not dead."

Silence.

"They're not," I say again, because if I stop saying it out loud, the truth might start to take shape.

Another pause from the woman on the other end. Then as if realizing then and there I am not going to accept her spewing bullshit: "We'll keep you updated."

The call ends. I stay sitting there the phone cold in my hand, disbelief burns through me like acid. My computer screen still blinking updates in front of me. The clock on my microwave is flashing at 10:21. The world doesn't fucking feel real. I feel myself slipping into that dark place I so often visit.

Leyla.

Cameron.

Dead?

No. No fucking way.

If this was over, I'd feel it.

And right now? All I felt was a lie.

AFTERWORD

BONUS CHAPTER
— FIGURE IT OUT
CHAPTER 23.5 - ZACK

This Tennessee heat has been unbearable, normally in October the weather isn't this bad, but I think the several monitors and computer servers aren't helping the fact that this room is a damn sauna. Sam's been on my ass about school forms and shit, and if you would have told me that I would be in charge of all of this I would have laughed. I'm 36 and with all that I've experienced in my life, the shit I'm dealing with right now doesn't even begin to scratch the surface of most of it.

I'm halfway through a cup of coffee that tastes like burnt regret when Cameron's name flashes on my screen. It's late and Cameron knows better than to call unless shit's on fire—figuratively or literally.

A feeling low in my stomach forms, and leaning back in my chair, I run my tattooed hand, my ring getting snagged on a knot in my definitely too long hair, as I answer without saying a word. His voice comes through tight, too controlled. "Z, we have a problem."

I sit up straight in my chair, already reaching for the secondary keyboard. He only gets like this when something's gone *very* wrong. Cameron's worked hard on keeping things together and this sounds like there's something more going on. There's a pause, just long enough to register the low thrum of the Maserati in the background.

Then he asks, "I had you looking into her past regarding the stalker. Any status update on that?"

I lean back again into my chair, mentally flipping through files like pages. "Nothing out of the ordinary. You already know everything about her father. The cemetery that he buried his victims in has been excavated. There are no children of his victims that would be targeting her. Her best friend checks out. The overbearing mother-figure detective as well. She has no contact with her adoptive or foster families."

I list the facts off like a grocery list, and I can practically *hear* the storm on the other end of the line, even if he's silent. His words hit me like a ton of bricks. Grabbing the pack of Marlboros I almost never use, I tap the cart on the palm of my hand, placing one in between my lips.

"Zack, someone took her."

The words don't register right away. My brain refuses to compute them. "What do you mean someone took her?" My mouth pops, open but I don't

Silence.

That's when I know, he's serious. He's about to go AWOL, and I am once again his singular voice of reason. Taking a deep breath, I know my plan, and what exactly I have to do, exactly what Cam needs right now.

"Cameron, we will find her," I say, voice flat, resolute. I don't do the whole emotional support thing. That's not me. But I've got *him*. Always have. Always will. "If something happens to her, Z, I promise you, I will stop at nothing to fucking kill everyone who played a hand in this. Everyone."

I don't doubt that for a second. Cameron has loved Leyla since they were kids, I remember being one of the leads in the group center, back when I was living up in Maplewood. Cameron's always talked about how Leyla was the one he would go to when he wanted to feel safe, feel whole. I never had that, but I respected him for the devotion he holds for her, always looking out for her, and being a good guy. I shake my head as I stare at the screen, waiting. The cursor blinks like a ticking clock.

This isn't just some job. This is my *Cameron*. This is his *Leyla*. I know that if something happened to Sam, I would stop at nothing to find and protect him.

And if someone took her? They're already dead. Pulling up my encrypted channel, I send out a message to my secondhand man, Lincoln, he's my go to guy, and if there's anyone, I trust with something like this it's Link. The cursor finally blinks out, replaced by a typing indicator.

LINCOLN: *On it. Send me coordinates. You running traffic cams or local feeds?*

I fire the info off in a burst, my fingers tapping in practiced rhythm across the keys. Lincoln's the only other person I trust to move as fast as I do. Maybe faster. The guy's a ghost—smart, surgical, and quiet as hell. Doesn't ask questions. That's why I use him. I flick between feeds. Parking lot. Entrance to her building. Side street. Camera angles jump around like they're trying to piss me off.

"Come on," I mutter, dragging through the last two hours of footage at four-times speed. Nothing. Empty. Normal. And then—

There.

I slam the space bar.

Tire marks. Fast exit. A white SUV—license plate partially obscured—pulling out of the lot like the devil himself is driving. Thirty seconds before that, a woman matching Leyla's build is struggling. One man. The male jumps out of the car he's wiry, twitchy. No face. No audio. The bastard knew where the blind spots were, but not *all* of them.

"Got you," I growl.

I rewind, slow it down frame-by-frame, tracing every detail. Leyla's phone hits the ground—screen still lit. One of the guys steps on it and walks away. Fucking amateur.

LINCOLN: *Sending you plate partials and a screenshot. Need facial recon and any flagged vehicle traffic near that complex in the last 48 hours. Focus on late-model white SUVs, missing plates, damage on the left taillight.*

I hit send and start my own trace, pulling into police scanners and private traffic logs they think are secure. They're not. Not from me.

My phone buzzes—Cam again, perfect timing as usual.

"Talk," I answer.

"You find anything?" His voice is sharper now. Less cold,

more... *shattered ice.* Dangerous in a different way. Cameron's normally calm demeanor has fully delved into a zone that reminds me a bit of his dad, I'd never say it but where Cameron goes when he's in the zone like this, even gives me pause.

"Yeah. White SUV. One male. Grabbed her and peeled out westbound at 7:42 PM. I'm working on getting a full plate. My guy's on facial ID."

A pause. Then with the tone that sent the hairs standing up on my arms. "How long before you get me something I can *hunt?*"

I chew the cigarette filter harder, jaw tight. "Give me twenty minutes, maybe less. You'll have names."

"I want locations."

"You'll have that too."

He hangs up without another word. That's fine. We don't need them.

The camera footage loops again in the corner of my screen, and I catch a small detail this time—a backpack strap on one of the guys. Yellow trim. I'm not letting anything go, if I had to guess this is someone she knew. Could be a hint. Could be a breadcrumb. Could be nothing.

But if it leads me to her, I'll burn down every database and strip every firewall between me and whoever the fuck touched her. No one hurts my family. While she's only known me as Mr. Zack from way back when, if she means this much to Cameron, as he's basically the only other one I have besides my actual brother, she in turn is family to me too.

I glance over at the far monitor. Lincoln's cursor is moving. Files are already loading in.

We're close.

Ping.

Lincoln: *Got it. Simon Maher, going through his search history now, but it seems like the SUV was last spotted on Corinne St, storage units.*

A zip file pops up on my screen. I send Link a thanks and immediately call Cam back.

His voice is more panicked now when he answers. "LEY-LA!?" I clear my throat ready to give him anything and everything I've got.

"It's not Leyla, but I've got an idea of where she might be," my calm voice trying to keep this as level as possible knowing that he's definitely not thinking with his head right now. "You're not gonna like what I'm about to tell you," I say, pacing in front of the monitors, teeth clenched tight around the end of a now thoroughly mangled cigarette filter. "I need you to stop moving around and think about it for a sec. With your head, not your fucking cock."

There's a beat of silence. Then I hear his breath catch, that subtle shift when his brain actually slows down. Cameron's at a door—*the* door—and he's waiting for a name. The name.

"Who is it, Z?" he asks, voice all shaken steel and wild adrenaline.

I can feel him holding still, frozen like a loaded weapon cocked and ready. I don't answer right away, because there's no clean way to say it. The name burns like acid on the way up.

"Zachary!" he shouts. "Who took my girl?!"

I close my eyes. Inhale.

"Simon Maher."

His name lands like a fucking bomb. There's a bated silence on the other end. And not the kind I like. There's fear now, buried beneath all that rage in Cameron's voice, but I know him well enough to hear the shift. This isn't just revenge. This is *personal failure* to him. He's blaming himself, stupid bastard.

"C, you there?" I ask, quieter this time.

Nothing.

So I keep going. "I tracked the car that took her. Ended up at a warehouse about ten minutes from where you are right now." I hear him move, he's anxiously moving around, probably just shifted his weight, maybe reaching for a weapon—and I can *feel* him about to demand the address. But I cut him off.

"Already sent it to you, brother," I say, a hint of a smirk curling the edge of my lips.

This is what we do. He moves. I guide. But even now, even in this mess, I have to keep him *grounded.* I know how easily he could slip. How close he's always been to becoming his father's legacy. The notoriety that follows him around has haunted him, and despite it all, he's stayed a truly good person.

"Don't get sloppy over this. You know who you are—and who you're not. Make him fucking pay for what he's done to her, got it? But don't lose yourself over it. You aren't your dad. Think logically. Don't do anything I wouldn't do."

...Which, to be fair, doesn't leave a lot off the table. But still. *He* knows what I mean.

I watch the screen as Cameron approaches the locked door —see the way his posture stiffens when he punches in his code.

"Oh, he's not going to know what fucking hit him," Cam growls through gritted teeth. "He's going to fucking regret ever touching what's mine. She's mine and he doesn't get to hurt her like that. Not my girl."

Good. Let the fury burn, but keep it focused.

"Be safe, Cameron," I say, adjusting a dial on the desk in front of me. "I've got eyes on you now, so you're not alone."

Right on cue, the drone feed flickers to life—thermal overlay glowing red against the cold night as it hovers over him. He looks up, eyes tracking it. Then, with all the grace of a teenage delinquent, he flips it off.

I snort. Can't help it. "Real mature."

His laughter follows mine—tight, short, but real. And needed. Fuck is it needed.

That's why I do this. Why I stay in the shadows and never ask for more than loyalty. Because this is what we've always done. He burns; I build. He moves, I see.

"I'm gonna take care of this," he says, calmer now. Focused. "I'll keep you in the know."

Then the line clicks dead.

I sit back, finally lighting the cigarette I've been chewing to death. The warehouse cameras are still dark. No digital footprint. That asshole think they're ghosts. But they don't have me on their side. I glance at the drone feed again, letting out the breath I wasn't even aware I was holding. I'm getting too old for this shit.,

"Go get your girl, C," I murmur. "I've got your six."

ACKNOWLEDGMENTS

I honestly don't even know where to begin with this, the fact that you're reading this means that I've actually completed my first book, which if you've been with me since the beginning, that means a lot. Like more than you could ever know. I have put my blood, sweat, and tears into this book. I am so thankful to have you as a reader and it means the literal world to me.

Michele, my dear dear love, my PA, my Editor, my artist extraordinaire. You came into my life after asking "who the fuck is that." And then suddenly you became someone who I simply cannot live without. You have made me so proud to know you and I truly would not be here without you. You helped me in more ways than one, and I don't mean in the ways of editing or anything of that sort. I mean you pushed me to be the very best version of myself every single day. You kept me on track and made sure that there would indeed be a book for me to finish. You're incredible, talented and truly the most inspiring and incredible people.

Aleesia, my adoring mistress/girlfriend since the title changes every single day, but I wouldn't have it literally any other way. You are such a bright light in my life and I am so so so thankful for you. Who would have known a silly little book series would bring me so many incredible friends (thank you Penn Cole). I love you to the moon and back and I'm honestly so so so thankful for you. You are one of the greatest people I've known and I can't wait to see where our friendship goes.

Kim, my british beauty, my girlie pop, my love. I am so thankful that our paths have crossed and I'm truly so thankful to have you in my life. I don't know what I would do without your sunshine smile and bubbly personality. You're incredible and please, never change. I love you.

To my friends: I owe you everything

Camille, the literal reason this book exists. You were my first ARC, my first author friend that I made and I am so lucky to have you in my life. I love you literally so much and I love our chaos conversations. You are one of my best friends and I am so lucky to have you as not only a friend but as someone who has been there from day one of this silly little book. Also I wouldn't have been able to do this without you. You're my literal hero. I love you.

Katie, my first book friend I met in person. The way I am so so so thankful for you in my life. You're an incredible person that I am so lucky to have you in my life. Whether it be telling you that Henri is the best character or you judging my questionable book taste. To being a fellow spoonie with me, I love you and thank you for sticking through this all with me. (Thank you Penn Cole again 😂)

Gina, hey bestie. I couldn't have done this without you, and I am honestly so thankful these silly little books brought us together. I love you so much. Thanks for putting up with my annoying ass. I am so thankful our paths have crossed in this lifetime and I will eternally know my life is better because you're in it.

Mariah, my GOD. I owe you literally everything. You answered every single question, no matter the time of day, or day of the week. I am so thankful for you and I don't know what I would have done without you. PS you're hot. Also I hope you know this is all your fault that I'm not absolutely obsessed with KPOP.

Stella, my beautiful friend. I am so so so thankful to have met you. Having fellow author friends has brightened my world and you are truly a gem among the rest. You're phenomenal and I'm so lucky to have you as a friend.

Ella, WOW HI FRIEND. I hope you know I had to go back and edit my acknowledgements, because you're truly such an incredible human. I am so thankful for you and your absolute unhinged love, and constant pride in literally telling the whole world about my book whenever we talked. The fact you went out of your way to make *that one thing that is SUPER SECRET and* then going and making the most incredible art, for little ol' me. Words do not begin to describe that. You're incredible, please never change. You're an incredible friend and I am truly so grateful to be your friend.

Also to **Janet**, my number one fan at work. You are the greatest human, and though I acted like a fool each time, I am so thankful for you always telling people about my book. You are a true joy to this world and deserve only the best.

To my beta and ARC readers, every single one of you is so

freaking special to me and I'm so thankful for you and your time and energy that went into reading this little book of mine. Without you there wouldn't be a book, and for that I am eternally thankful. I truly hope you all have enjoyed taking this journey with me, and I am so grateful for each and everyone of you.

The book community – thank you. You have become my family over these last couple months and you made all of this possible. I owe you everything as there is nothing without all of you. You are all my world and I owe you everything. Never change, stay weird and know that I will always love you. This entire journey has been life changing and I have lived and learned so much while publishing this book and I wouldn't change a single thing.

ABOUT THE AUTHOR

Mae Roberts was born in the Midwest and spends 98% of her time reading and making friends on the internet. The Moments You Miss is her debut, theShe has many more fun projects in her pipeline, so if you want to stay up to date, connect with Mae online!

Instagram: @authormaeroberts

E-Mail: authormaeroberts@outlook.com

9 798999 124814